BURIED SECRETS

A.D. ELLIS

1

DRAKE

"Tell me what you saw." Drake Lewis, homicide detective with the Indianapolis Metropolitan Police Department, poised his pen on the small leather-bound notebook and ignored the sting of the icy Indiana spring wind against his cheeks.

"Came in early to get the old concrete broken up. New foundation being poured today." Chuck jerked a thumb over his shoulder at his concrete truck.

The men stood outside of the crime scene area, but close enough that Drake could see all of what was going on. He frowned. "When was this concrete poured?"

"Couldn't have been more than a year ago, probably even less. Few months maybe." Chuck shrugged. "But the apartment complex is expanding. So, this had to be torn out for the new concrete."

"Do you know who poured the old concrete? What was it for?" Drake fired off questions as he scribbled on his notepad.

"Looked like an amateur job. Probably some residents

got permission to make a basketball slab or something." Chuck kicked at a rock as he walked closer to the crime scene.

"So, you came to break up and remove the old concrete. Tell me about that." Drake spoke as he finished writing one sentence only to begin a new one about what Chuck began to say.

"Concrete wasn't busting the way it usually does. Should have been a quick and easy job. Bust it up, gather the pieces, and move 'em out of the way." Chuck adjusted his winter cap as his gaze surveyed the scene.

"But you ran into trouble?" *Duh, man, yeah I'd say body parts buried in concrete would be considered trouble.*

Chuck huffed. "You could say that. I didn't recognize the arm at first. But the leg definitely scared the shit out of me. Called 911 immediately."

"You call anyone else?" Drake narrowed his eyes.

"Called the construction foreman. Woke him up, but he'll be here soon."

"What do you know, from your experience, about body parts in concrete?"

Chuck scratched an ear. "They'd need to be anchored down. If not, they could float to the surface before the concrete set up. From the pieces I pulled up, looks like they were anchored with rebar. Probably buried just enough under the dirt and anchored before the concrete was poured. The slab was done pretty shoddily. Wouldn't have passed inspection for a building. Likely had a lot of air bubbles and unevenness. But probably decent enough for a kids' basketball court."

"Okay. Stick around for questions as they come up. The crew may also need your help in breaking up the remaining concrete. We'll have to get some trucks in here to transport the slab to the lab." Drake made one last note. Up next on his interview list was the Shadow Woods Apartments complex property manager.

Drake scanned the area.

A pick-up truck pulled into the apartment building's front entrance and rolled through the soft mud to the back of the property.

A man climbed from the truck.

A man Drake recognized.

Fuck.

Liam Walters. Even looking as if he just rolled from bed, the man was gorgeous.

They'd met a few times on Mass Ave. in downtown Indianapolis. The last time Drake had seen Liam was about a month ago. Drinks and dancing were enjoyed and then Drake *thoroughly* enjoyed his night in Liam's bed. Flashes of that night flitted through his head, and he fought the urge to pinch the bridge of his nose. Liam was hot as sin, but Drake kept his personal life separate from his professional life. Completely separate. And professional life always trumped personal life.

Recognition lit Liam's eyes, but Drake shut him down with a quick shake of his head.

Liam's nostrils flared, but he played along. "Liam Walters, construction foreman." Liam held out a hand for Drake to shake.

"Morning, Mr. Walters." Drake shook his hand briskly. Drake ignored the heat in his hand from where Liam had touched him. "Your man was just telling me about the unexpected items he found while busting up the concrete. What can you tell me about this property?"

Liam dropped Drake's hand before turning to greet Chuck. "Morning, Chuck, thanks for calling. Sorry you had such a shocking experience." Liam turned to Drake, his light brown hair flipping up at the edges of his beanie cap. Blue eyes flashing, Liam studied Drake for a moment. "Probably can't tell you as much as the property manager other than Shadow Woods is one of the largest complexes on the south side of Indianapolis. With this expansion, it will be the largest. It's one of the area's nicer complexes. The project we bid on will double their spread and occupancy. We're slated to start today which is why Chuck was here. We needed the old slab gone so we could start work on pouring the foundations." Liam clasped both hands behind his head, his shirt riding up from the waistband of his jeans to show his pale skin and that enticing trail of brown hair. "This will put us behind for sure."

Drake clenched his teeth and looked away from Liam's skin. He didn't need the distraction. "We'll be out of your hair as quickly as possible, but we won't leave until we have all that we need. Perhaps you can start work on a different location of the project."

"Yeah, we'll just change the whole project, no problem." Liam huffed and rolled his eyes.

Drake surveyed the crime scene and surrounding area. "Looks like most of the expansion will be far enough toward the back of the property that most of the current residents shouldn't be too bothered, huh?"

"That's the plan." Liam shrugged.

"Do you have the contact info for the property manager?"

"Yeah, Eric Cooper." Liam pulled out his phone and pulled up Mr. Cooper's name. "317-555-3149."

Drake scribbled the name and number. He nodded dismissively at Liam and punched the digits into his phone. "Is this Eric Cooper?" Drake spoke sternly into the phone. "This is Detective Drake Lewis with IMPD Homicide. I need to speak to you. Are you able to come to Shadow Woods or would you rather meet me at the station? We have an open homicide case, and I need information from you as the property manager." Drake took Cooper's quick reply of *I'll be right there* to mean Shadow Woods would work fine. He disconnected the phone.

"So, not the greatest situation, but it's nice to see you again," Liam began quietly as Chuck wandered away.

Drake coughed and glanced around before continuing. "Not here. We can get coffee or something later." What the hell was he doing? Drake had no reason to invite Liam for coffee. Questions about Liam's crew and the apartment complex area. That was all. Drake didn't do repeats with men he hooked up with. Repeats had too much potential to get messy.

Liam's face scrunched up before a look of dawning spread across his beautiful features. "Ah, gotcha. Your buddies at Homicide don't know you're gay."

"Would you shut your fucking mouth?" Drake hissed and glanced around again before turning back to Liam. "I said coffee. Later. I have work to do. I'm guessing you do too."

Drake turned back to watch the crew work the scene on the other side of the tape. But he could still sense Liam's presence behind him. He was fairly confident the victim hadn't been killed at this spot—too out in the open for a murder *and* keeping a body around until it could be buried in concrete—but they needed to collect as much evidence as possible. And every single piece of concrete needed to be taken back to the lab along with all the soil containing the body parts, hair, nails, clothing, everything. Whoever got the job of piecing that body back together was not going to be pleased. Or maybe they'd be thrilled. Drake knew some of their lab geeks got off on that kind of stuff.

"Holy shit, what's going on?" A man spoke from beside Drake, causing the detective to startle.

"Who are you?" Drake demanded.

"Eric Cooper. Property manager." Eric stuck out his hand.

"Detective Lewis, Homicide." Drake shook his hand. "You know Liam Walters."

Eric and Liam shook hands.

"How'd you get here so quick?" Drake frowned.

"I live on property." Eric shrugged.

Drake raised a brow. "And you didn't see the activity and wonder what was up before I called you?" He crossed his arms over his chest.

Eric blushed. "I was up late fixing a leaky pipe for a resident. Damn water was everywhere. After I got the pipe tightened, I brought my wet vac over and helped vacuum the water from her carpet. Damn exhausted once I got back to my place and I sleep like the dead. And my place is at the far end of the complex, farthest away from here as you can get. Didn't hear a thing, sorry." Eric ran a hand over his face as he turned toward Liam. "How far is this going to set us behind?"

"Depends on how quickly they can get this all cleaned up and clear us to start work on this portion." Liam pulled up something on his phone. "Based on these plans, we should be able to work around the issue at least for a while. Won't be convenient, but we'll make it work."

"Not like you have a choice. Dead bodies take precedence over building new apartments." Drake slapped his notebook against his thigh. The spring weather had not turned warm yet, and his ears were tingling in the cold, biting wind. "So, Cooper, tell me about the property."

Eric cleared his throat and pulled his baseball cap down before shoving both hands in his pockets. "I've only been property manager for a few months. I've lived here about a year maybe. Took the job recently to get my mind off some bad shit. The expansion project has been in the works for a while. Glad to get it started. We've got a lot of people on a waiting list. Being within Indianapolis, but as far outside of downtown as possible is a huge draw. We're fairly priced too."

"When did this slab go in? What was it for?" Drake gestured toward the busted-up concrete.

Eric furrowed his brow. "Well now, I don't rightly recall. It was put in for basketball I think, at least that's what it ended up being used for. I think it was poured about three months ago? Got used a lot until the rim got bent. I think the kids were hoping to get another rim soon so they could get back to their games."

"Who poured the court?" Drake took notes as he spoke.

"Some residents. They got permission from the previous property manager—he was pretty lax with shit like that. I definitely wouldn't have allowed it, but my understanding is this area wasn't included in the original expansion plans. But the newer version of the project ended up using this area. So the slab had to be broken up." Eric tugged at his hat again. "I'm sorry if it's out of line, but can I ask what was found? Having a homicide detective on my property is something I'm going to have to explain to the residents."

"Body parts, anchored under the concrete." Drake didn't mince words—probably shouldn't have given the info, but the construction crew who found the body were already talking amongst themselves. And the media was already hanging around; much of the information would be public knowledge soon. "The department will give you the information needed to inform the residents. They will likely be asked to come forward with any details they could provide. I'm not speaking officially, but I doubt the victim was killed here and I'm even more sure the suspect won't come back while police are crawling around. I don't expect there's any immediate danger to your residents."

"Do you know who it is?" Eric pointed his chin toward the taped off area.

"Nah, we'll hopefully get prints and run them through the system." Drake had seen a lot of the body parts in question. Definitely didn't look like a young person based on size. But male or female was still up in the air.

"Will prints still be there? How long do you think the body has been there?" Eric removed his hands from his coat pockets and wrapped them around his waist.

"Well, the body was likely put there when the concrete was poured." Drake fought the urge to roll his eyes and whisper, duh, under his breath. "But, we don't yet know how long the body had been dead before it was buried under the slab. As for the prints, as long as they weren't burned or bleached off, we should be able to get a good set."

"Whoa, so you think the guys who poured the concrete put the body there?" Eric's eyes were wide.

"Maybe, maybe not. Pieces could have been put under the dirt before the concrete was poured." Drake opened his notebook to scribble a note to ask the lab. "We'll get it figured out. Don't worry."

"Okay, glad you know what you're doing. I need to contact my boss and let him know what's going on." Eric checked his phone. "Do you need me here right now?"

"Not this second, but make yourself available through the day and the week."

Eric nodded and then headed toward the opposite end of the complex.

Liam finished up something at his truck and trudged his work boots through the sticky mud to stand beside Drake. "I'll readjust the plans for this site. You let me know when you want to grab that coffee."

Drake grunted.

He was used to taking orders from his ex-military father. But he didn't take orders well from anyone else. Liam needed to understand they'd get that coffee when and where Drake decided.

His insides itched with the anxiety of getting prints and figuring out the victim's identity. More than that, Drake wanted to land the murderer. The last case he'd worked was eventually sent to the Cold Case Unit and Drake did *not* plan to give this one up.

Detective Sam Mathers worked between Homicide and

the Cold Case Unit. He rode Drake hard and never passed up a chance to rub Drake's face in an unsolved case.

Sam was also very much too interested in Drake's dating life.

"Lewis, I never see you out with a girl. What's up with that? You playing for the other team?"

"Dumbass. Do you ever see me out with a guy? No. Why? Because I keep my personal life private, the way it should be."

People were more accepting and open these days. Drake could have come out when he joined the force. But now, as a thirteen-year-veteran at the age of thirty-five, revealing that aspect of himself was too hard. How did he even bring that up? And really, whose business was it anyway? No one's business. Period. Solving cases, keeping people safe, and helping victims' families find closure were Drake's top priorities.

DRAKE FINISHED up with the crew at the scene. "I'll check in once I'm back in the office." He smacked a hand onto the shoulder of the crew member heading up the scene.

He found Liam pouring over a digital tablet and an unrolled blueprint plan at the bed of his work truck. "You got time for that coffee now?"

Liam stood from his hunched over position and frowned at Drake. "Look like I have time? Look like I'm just studying the prints and plans for the hell of it, waiting on you to deem your time worthy to speak to me?"

Drake gritted his jaw and ran a hand through his hair. "Listen, sorry, I realize you're busy. I can take a short break now; my lieutenant requires I take breaks and lunches or I'd work twenty-four seven. If you're available, let me buy you a coffee." Drake knew he had people at the department who were already following up with missing persons, checking in with the lab about what was discovered after canvasing the area, and pouring over security camera footage. He'd get full reports from them when he got back to the office. He was lucky the people who worked with him and under him were very good at their jobs and could be trusted to do thorough work. They would get him the most up-to-date and pertinent information regarding the case. Their work combined with his own was always better than what he could do on his own even if he hated to admit it. A few years ago, his lieutenant had demanded Drake take breaks *and* allow a team to do some of the work on his cases. Lieutenant Simms had slapped Drake on the back and said, "You either do this or you're going to work yourself into a nervous breakdown or stroke. I won't have that on my watch."

Liam pulled off his cap, ruffled his wild brown hair, and set the hat back in place. Frowning, he spoke. "Your apology is crap. But it's cold out here and we're pushed back from starting at least a week now. Sure, I'll let you buy me coffee." He winked.

Drake felt heat shoot straight to his groin. He'd casually dated a few men. He'd fucked *a lot* of men. Liam was one he hadn't forgotten. In fact, if he played his cards right, he could possibly keep their little fling going for a bit longer. Nothing wrong with an enjoyable one-night stand lasting a little longer than one night.

"Meet me at Beans and Things."

"We could ride together," Liam suggested.

"Nah, I'll need my car to head back to the office." It was one thing to be seen with Liam late at night on Mass Ave, but Drake had no real reason to have coffee with Liam in the middle of a work day. Better to not be seen arriving at Beans and Things *together*.

Liam pursed his lips, nodded his head, and gave a little wave.

Fifteen minutes later, Drake pocketed his keys and pushed his way against the icy blast of wind toward Beans and Things. Damn, winter just wasn't letting go this year. The little coffee and more shop was located at the corner between two quiet streets with an alley on the back side and a dry cleaner to the left. The concrete exterior was brightly painted with all things coffee, tea, baked goods, and happiness.

"Should have worn a hat," Liam offered when Drake entered the tiny vestibule of the building.

"Forgot it at home," Drake mumbled. "What do you want? I'll grab the drinks while you get the table."

"Damn, you're bossy. Nice trait in bed, but..." Liam trailed off when Drake shot daggers his way. "Black coffee, please."

Drake's ears burned as they warmed in the cozy coffee shop. He studied the menu while trying to forget Liam's words about him being bossy in bed. Damn right he was bossy in bed. Nothing better than getting a sexy willing man under him to take those commands—to take him. *Fuck.* Stop thinking about Liam in bed.

He finally wound his way through the shop, two steaming clay mugs in hand, and found the far corner table Liam had snagged. "Did you want cream or sugar?"

Liam's brow rose. "The handful of cream and sugar in your hand isn't to share? Damn. Guess you like a little coffee with your sweet cream." He took the sturdy mug and sniffed it appreciatively.

Drake rolled his eyes and plopped down, glad Liam had left the corner seat open so he could see the whole shop. Having his back to the door at any shop or restaurant always bothered him. He doctored up his coffee and stirred before taking a drink.

"So, we didn't do a whole lot of talking the last time we were together," Liam began.

Drake clenched his jaw and willed his cock not to take notice of the memory of Liam spread out before him flashing through his head.

"Tell me, what brought you to law enforcement?" Liam blew gently on his coffee before taking a tiny sip.

"Watched some bad shit go down when I was little. Police officers saved me. Got the bad guy. Grew up knowing that rules were important, and I wanted to get the bad guys too." Drake shrugged. Watching his mother murdered in a robbery gone wrong would haunt him for the rest of his life. But Drake had sworn to spend the rest of his life righting wrongs and putting the bad guys away. "What about you? Why construction?"

Liam chewed the inside of his cheek. "I mostly grew up in the foster system. It sucked, but got me away from the bad shit at home. The dad at one of my last foster homes did construction. He'd let me go to the sites sometimes. I got hooked. The rest is history."

Drake didn't push, but he definitely noticed Liam's jaw clench when he spoke of the *bad shit at home*. Abused?

Druggie parents? Neglected? Not Drake's place to ask, but he'd seen how bad the *bad shit* could be.

"You enjoy it?" Drake asked before sipping his coffee.

Liam nodded. "Yeah, I do. It's good money, I'm pretty good at it, and it keeps me moving." He sipped his coffee. "What about you? You like what you do?"

"I was one of the best patrol officers of my academy class. But I wanted more. Wanted to catch the scumbags out murdering innocent people. Climbed the ranks fairly quickly. Got some awards and applied to Homicide. One of the youngest homicide detectives on the force."

"Impressive. But do you *like* what you do?" Liam persisted.

Drake drank his coffee. "I like knowing I've put a bad guy away and given a victim's family closure. The shit I see isn't fun. I wish there was no need for me. But getting to the bottom of a case is rewarding. So, do I *like* what I do? I find it fulfilling even if I wish there was no need for homicide detectives."

"Fair enough." Liam let the subject drop. "Based on the way you shut me up at the complex, I'm guessing the guys in your unit don't know you're gay?"

"It's not like I lie and say I'm *not* gay. It just never comes up." Drake never liked this conversation and always felt the need to defend himself. "Does your crew know you're gay?"

Liam nodded. "I even dated one of them for a while. But we decided we were better as friends."

Damn. Totally didn't expect that.

"And none of them give you a hard time?"

Could Drake put up with the constant hounding he'd

get at work? The teasing? Would he lose the respect he'd worked so hard to earn?

"I mean, it's not something we talk about on a daily basis. Not all the guys know, the newer ones learn eventually. The temps may not ever know. I'm happy with who I am. There's enough shit in my past to weigh on me. I don't need the fact that I like guys being one of my issues." Liam shrugged.

"Wish it was that easy for me." Drake really did.

"It could be. You probably built it up so huge in your head when in reality revealing who you are wouldn't be that terrible." Liam stared at Drake over his coffee cup.

"You don't know the unit I work with." Drake shook his head.

"So, you think the crew you work with doesn't know a single gay man? You think there's *no way* any of them are hiding the same secret? You can't begin to tell me that there aren't LGBTQ people in the IMPD as a whole." Liam swirled the coffee around in this mug.

"I'm sure there are. I keep to myself, it's not really my business to get into their lives. And my life isn't their business."

"So, in other words, you have very few friends on the force or in your unit. And you hide yourself behind gay bars and random hook-ups."

Drake clenched his jaw. This man didn't know him. He didn't know the stress that came with Drake's job. Didn't know the importance of keeping personal and professional life separate.

"Why did you ask me to coffee?" Liam plodded on.

Drake shrugged. "Seeing you reminded me of our night together."

"And you wanted a repeat?" Liam cocked a brow.

"I can't do anything serious, but I thought we had fun. Maybe let whatever it is run its course?" It was the best Drake could offer. He didn't do serious relationships. Never had. Serious relationships got in the way of work and turned messy.

"So, fuck buddies?"

Drake glanced at Liam, trying to get a read. "Compatible partners who enjoy each other's company and sex for as long as it lasts?" Drake offered, knowing his description was no better than Liam's.

"I'm down." Liam drained his coffee. "Want to squeeze in a nooner and then make firm plans for next time?"

Drake glanced around the shop. Did anyone hear that? "Keep it down." He knew Liam's place was close.

As if he read Drake's mind, Liam offered. "Keep your car out back. I'll drive. I can drop you off here on my way back to the site."

"I've got less than an hour." His lieutenant *did* demand Drake take breaks. This could count.

"Let's go." Liam jingled his keys.

Less than ten minutes later, they arrived at Liam's place. "Make yourself at home. Just gonna use the restroom and freshen up a bit." Liam gestured toward the neutral colored and simply decorated living room as he removed his shoes at the door. "Beer's probably not a good idea, but there's water, juice, or pop in the fridge."

Drake acknowledged the offer with a nod and a grunt as he slipped his shoes off, as well. He watched Liam disappear down the narrow hall to the bedroom. They had started their first hookup on the couch before eventually moving to the bed. Would they begin on the bed today?

Drake glanced at the brown leather couch and recalled Liam bent over the back, ass spread wide, and determined the couch would do just fine.

He'd checked in with Lieutenant Simms on the drive to fill him in on what Drake knew, what the team was working on, and to go over a statement the Public Relations Department was working on for the media. Drake shared a few hunches and possible leads with the lieutenant and assured the man he was taking a short break before coming back to the office. Drake knew he was given a lot of freedom to work cases the way he saw best fit. Lieutenant Simms trusted Drake to do his job.

He silenced his work phone. If his personal phone rang, he'd know it was an emergency.

He popped into the small restroom just off the entryway. It was only a toilet and sink, but hot water, soap, and a washcloth would do just fine in a pinch. Drake washed his face before cleaning the rest of his necessary pieces. He paused before tossing the damp cloth in the tiny hamper. If Liam was anything like Drake, he wouldn't check the hamper for months and the damp cloth would be gross and mildewed long before then. He carried the cloth with him and met Liam in the kitchen.

"Didn't want to put this in the hamper since it's wet. Where should I toss it?" Drake held up the cloth.

"Just throw it in that bucket under the sink. It's got washcloths and rags and sponges I need to wash soon anyway." Liam pointed toward the cabinet and Drake obeyed.

Liam wrapped his arms around Drake's waist and kissed his neck. "We don't have much time, you ready?"

Drake growled and rocked his thickening cock into

Liam's. "Hell yeah." He kissed Liam roughly, enjoying the minty taste on Liam's tongue. "No fair, I couldn't brush my teeth."

"You taste like coffee, no worries." Liam ran his tongue along Drake's bottom lip before backing away and pulling off his shirt which he tossed toward the general vicinity of the hallway. His well-worn jeans soon followed. "Better catch up," Liam taunted.

Drake unbuttoned his dress shirt, glad he hadn't bothered with a tie that morning. He pulled his shirt from his pants and hung it on the back of the recliner next to the couch. His slacks were next, folded neatly on the back of the chair.

"So precise," Liam teased and ran his hands up Drake's torso, pausing to play with his nipples.

"I have to go back to the office, I can't look like I just romped in the hay," Drake grumped, but quickly forgot his argument when Liam tongued his nipple.

Liam maneuvered them toward the couch. "Next time, let's plan for more time to do things properly." He pushed Drake's ass against the back of the couch before dropping to his knees. Liam slid Drake's underwear down his long, sinewy legs, groaning when Drake's cock sprung up to meet him. "Mmmm, just what I wanted for lunch," Liam whispered, eyes on Drake's while he tongued the leaking slit.

Drake gripped Liam's hair and fed his length between Liam's lips. "Suck me."

Liam eagerly obliged.

When Drake's balls drew up tight, he pushed Liam from his dick. "Bend over the couch," Drake commanded as he grabbed a condom from his wallet and rolled it on. "You got any lube?"

"I prepped a little. Spit's fine if you need more." Liam bent over the back of the couch and threw a glance over his shoulder as he spread his legs and offered Drake his ass.

Fuck. So hot.

Drake teased Liam's ass with a finger and found him plenty slick. Another day, he'd take time for teasing and stretching and foreplay, but today was only about the sex. Drake lined up his cock and nudged Liam's hole. He pressed gently, a tiny bit at a time, until Liam's body gave in and allowed Drake's invasion. Drake paused, letting Liam's muscles adjust, then gripped Liam's hips and began thrusting with a slow and heavy rhythm.

"Jack yourself," Drake commanded as his thighs slapped the back of Liam's legs. His balls tightened with each deep slide into Liam's ass. "Fuck, move to the couch."

Drake moved their coupling quickly to the front of the couch and sat slouched down so Liam could straddle his hips. "Ride me."

Liam gripped Drake's cock and positioned himself to take the hard length deep. "Ahhh, fuck, so good."

Drake reached for Liam's dick and jacked him while pumping into Liam's tight, hot ass. "Come for me. Shoot it all over me."

Liam moaned and batted Drake's hand out of the way so he could pump his own cock to completion. "Fuck, fuck. You're so damn hot, I'm gonna come." Liam threw his head back and groaned and shot his load all over Drake's stomach and chest.

Drake gripped Liam's hips hard enough he knew the man's pale flesh would bruise and held him tight while his powerful thrusts rocked up into Liam's ass. One final pump and Drake exploded, spilling thick, hot spurts into the condom. Liam's ass milked Drake's throbbing cock.

Drake pulled Liam close and kissed him. The man was an amazing fuck. If Drake was looking for more than casual, he'd think about making this thing with Liam more permanent. But Drake needed easy and casual. "That was fucking fantastic," Drake whispered against Liam's mouth. "We have to make sure we can do that several more times, at least until one of us gets tired of it."

"Agreed." Liam kissed him. "As much as I hate to say it, we better get cleaned up. We both have jobs to get back to."

Drake groaned. "You're right."

They washed up and dressed before rushing out to Liam's truck.

"Give me your phone, I'll put my number in. Text me and we'll get something worked out for later." Drake held out his hand for Liam's phone as Liam drove them back to the coffee shop.

"I may see you around the work site at least for the time being, right?" Liam asked as they pulled into the back lot of Beans and Things.

"Yeah, it's likely. But I'm talking about more than just a brief conversation."

"Got it. And you don't want me acting like there's any connection between us, at least at the job?"

"There's not really a *connection* between us. Just casual sex until one of us moves on, right?" Drake honestly hated the way that sounded, but he didn't have any other option to offer.

"Yeah," Liam bit out. "I'll see you around."

Drake fought the urge to say more, but just slapped Liam's shoulder. "Thanks for the ride." He climbed from the truck and gave Liam a quick wave before heading to his car.

2

LIAM

"Boss man, I gotta head over to the other two worksites first thing in the morning," the cement truck operator, Dave, hollered from his truck window. "I'll be over here around noon."

"Why are you working those sites?" Liam asked.

"One of the truck guys dislocated his shoulder. I'm picking up extra runs. Not gonna turn down the money, ya know?"

"Gotcha. Okay, see you tomorrow." Liam waved.

"When do you think the work you're supposed to get done will actually get started?" A voice sounded behind Liam.

Liam turned to see the apartment property manager, Eric with a flushed face and crossed arms. "Well, a police investigation is sure to slow things down. Not much we can do about that. We'll do all the work we can while working around the case."

Eric cursed and scuffed his shoe in the damp dirt.

"Man, listen. I get that it's frustrating, but it is what it is. No one's fault, other than the dumbass who buried a body under a concrete slab."

"Yeah, well, I better see your crew busting ass any time I look over this way," Eric grumbled before walking away.

Liam raised his brows and watched the man's retreating back. "What the hell crawled up his ass?"

"He's been having a rough time." Chris, one of Liam's crew, removed his cap and ran a hand through his hair. Chris lived in the area and knew a lot of people at the Shadow Woods apartments. "Some family stuff dealing with a foster kid and Department of Child Services, and then a death in the family from what I've heard."

"Damn," Liam breathed. "That's a lot. Anyone would be fucked up with that going on."

"Yeah." Chris grimaced. "Hey, can you keep that info quiet? The grapevine is strong and useful, but probably not any of my business to be sharing."

"No worries, I'll keep quiet. But thanks for the information. Helps me to know he's not just being an asshole." Liam watched Eric as he continued his walk to the front of the complex.

Liam didn't know Eric well. Didn't really know him at all. But the story Chris told him earlier that day stuck with Liam. As a kid who grew up in an abusive home, he had a pretty good understanding of how screwed up the foster care system was. While it *could* be a lifesaver for many, it wasn't always the answer to a kid's problems.

If Eric's family had been dealing with the stress of DCS visits and fostering, Liam knew the guy was rightfully tense. Add the death of a family member on top of that, it made sense why Eric was shitty.

He loved his mom beyond measure, but Liam learned

quickly that she had some major issues. Mom wasn't like the other mothers. Mom never picked him over her latest boyfriend or drugs. While his mother never hit him, she was very neglectful, especially when she was high.

Department of Child Services was called on her more times than he could count. Overworked and underpaid social workers would come to investigate. They must have also been blind. Or maybe completely incapable of filing a report or following up, because nothing happened.

Until him.

Scariest motherfucker Liam had ever seen in his life.

Liam realized the new guy was bad news the second he saw him.

And that night, the guy didn't go to Liam's strung-out mom. He went to Liam's room.

The pain and fear and shame of that night was forever burned in Liam's head and on his heart.

But that man was the reason Liam was finally put into the foster care system. Many of the homes he stayed in were barely tolerable, but they kept him away from the abuse. Then, best miracle of Liam's short life, he was placed in a true home. A mom and dad who actually seemed happy to have him there. They took care of Liam *and* spent time with him. His foster dad taught Liam everything he knew about construction.

The foster care system was beyond fucked up. That much was true then and likely even more true now. But that system, the one failing so many, actually saved Liam and gave him a new start.

But the daily news was overflowing with kids who weren't as lucky as Liam. Kids who would never get that new start.

Later, when Liam's phone buzzed, he was surprised to see Drake's name on the screen. "Hello?"

"You want to grab drinks and dinner tonight?" Drake asked curtly on the other side of the phone.

Liam was beginning to realize that Drake wasn't just an emotionally unattached hard ass with him, that just seemed to be his personality in general. "Sounds good. Want to go out or stay in?"

"Let's do drinks out and see about dinner after." Drake's voice mixed with the sound of a machine.

"You at the office?"

"Yeah. Getting some reports printed."

"The apartment complex case?" Liam figured Drake likely worked more than just one case at a time at least in some capacity.

"Yeah," Drake mumbled over the sound of ruffling pages. "So, six? I'll swing by your place. That okay?"

"Sounds good. See you then."

At six that evening, Liam watched from the front window as Drake pulled up to the apartment. Liam popped into the bathroom to run product through his light brown hair. He knew his hair would do the *naturally messy* thing on its own, but the product helped keep it looking decent instead of journeying from naturally messy to finger in a light socket crazy. Liam washed his hands and went to the front hall to put on his shoes and gather his coat, keys, and phone.

What was taking Drake so long?

Liam glanced out the window and saw Drake just sitting in his car.

His phone buzzed.

. . .

DRAKE: I'm here. Can you come on down?

LIAM ROLLED HIS EYES. "Coming to the door too chivalrous for you, Lewis?" More like Drake was too afraid to be seen picking Liam up for anything that may have even slightly resembled a date. Pocketing his phone and keys, Liam threw his coat on and headed down the stairs.

"Hey," he said as he climbed in Drake's car.

"Hey," Drake mumbled. "Figured we'd save time if I didn't come up."

"Mmmhm," Liam breathed. "Where we going?"

"Thought maybe Tini's and Metro for drinks. We can eat at Metro if you want. Or grab food and take it home. Maybe watch a movie?" Drake pulled from Liam's complex and melded into traffic.

"Sounds good. Maybe grab dinner at The Pub? Love their food." Liam's stomach growled at the mention of food.

Drake chuckled. "Do I need to feed you first?"

Liam's cheeks heated. "Nah, drinks will fill me up for a while." He glanced at Drake's profile. Dark stubble on his firm jawline. A perfect chin and almost perfect nose, just slightly crooked. Black hair that appeared to have more of a mind of its own than Liam's.

Liam chuckled. He would place money that Drake cursed and bossed his hair around every morning.

Drake turned deep brown eyes toward Liam. "What?"

Liam shook his head. "Nothing."

Drake grumbled something, but they were nearing Mass Avenue and Drake ordered Liam to help him look for parking.

They lucked out and found a newly vacated spot. Liam jumped out to pay the meter.

"I can pay my own parking," Drake stated.

"You drove, I'll pay for parking."

They spent about an hour in Tini's drinking at a small, dark table away from everyone. Drake and Liam spoke of random things ranging from Liam's rent, Drake's lease on his car, the Pride parade that took place each year in June, and they even discussed the damn weather. But it was comfortable and easy and Liam enjoyed every second of it.

Liam chastised himself as Drake excused himself to the restroom, *Don't let this mean too much, Walters. Drake isn't willing or able to offer anything more than some casual dates and meaningless sex. Don't ever forget that.*

Then why are you even giving him the time?

Liam ran a hand over his face. *Damned if I know. I can't get a good read on it, but I like the guy for some reason. Maybe it's knowing Drake had a rough childhood similar to me. Maybe it's something I'll never be able to explain. Maybe it's wishful thinking. But I feel a connection to him.*

Liam sighed heavily and drained the rest of his drink before Drake returned.

"You ready?" Drake emerged from the stairway next to their table.

"Yep." Liam shrugged into his jacket and followed Drake to the door. It didn't skip Liam's notice that Drake led them to the less occupied side of the bar and out the door where they wouldn't need to speak to anyone.

Once they were settled at Metro, drinks and appetizers ordered, Liam spoke up. "Doesn't it get old always having to hide?"

"What do you mean? Hide?" Drake frowned.

"Avoiding coming to my door, sitting at the farthest darkest table, using the less busy door. I'm actually surprised you're not in a hat and sunglasses."

"I'm out in public, aren't I?" Drake demanded. "I spoke to people at Tini's. I just said hi to two people here at this bar. So, I don't like to socialize a ton. Doesn't mean I'm hiding."

"And if someone from IMPD walked in here right now?" Liam cocked a brow.

"I may not even recognize them." Drake shrugged. "Contrary to popular belief, members of the force don't know every other member."

"Let's say a guy walked in here with his date and spoke directly to you. 'Detective Lewis, hi, nice to see you. I'm so-and-so from whatever unit. This is my boyfriend.' What would you do with that?" Liam pushed.

Their waiter brought drinks and food at that exact moment.

"Let's just drop it, huh?" Drake grumbled.

Liam drew in a deep breath. "For now. But you need to be better to yourself. You can't expect a stressful job to be the only thing that keeps you going for the rest of your life."

"It's worked so far." Drake forked a mozzarella stick from the plate. He tossed the stick onto Liam's plate and then shoveled some zucchini sticks onto the plate as well. "Eat up."

Liam rolled his eyes at the way Drake dismissed the conversation. For the time being.

About an hour later, they paid their bill and finished off their drinks.

"You want to eat at The Pub or take the food home?"

Drake asked as they headed out into the blast of cold, damp early Midwest spring.

"Let's just take it home. My place or yours?" Liam knew the general area where Drake lived, but he'd never been to Drake's home.

"Yours makes more sense."

Liam pressed his lips together. Sure his place made more sense. It really did. But he couldn't help but think it was just another way for Drake to keep Liam at arm's length.

Why do you care? You knew going into this that Drake didn't do relationships. If you can't handle that, walk now. Liam gritted his teeth and drew in a deep breath. *Maybe I'm a glutton for punishment. Maybe the romantic dreamer inside me thinks I'll be the one to break through to him. Or maybe I'm just a total idiot.*

They entered The Pub and Liam's mouth watered at the scent of fried food. The waitress took their to-go order and promised it would be up soon. Onion rings, two fish sandwiches, and a burger to split. Fries never traveled home well.

By the time they'd reached Liam's place, he was hungry again and glad they'd decided to chill at home rather than stay out. They kicked off their shoes and spread the feast on the coffee table.

"You want water? Pop?" Liam sauntered toward the kitchen.

"Water's good. Thanks."

Liam brought two bottles of water to the living room.

"I swear, The Pub has the best damn fish sandwich." Liam spoke around a bite of onion ring.

"The burger isn't bad, but the fish is amazing." Drake

chewed a bite of the burger and handed the other half to Liam.

"What movie you want to watch?" Liam turned on the television.

"Depends. Are we actually *watching* a movie?" Drake cocked a brow.

Liam chuckled. "Up to you. I'm game for whatever."

"Then I say turn on whatever you want, but don't plan on watching anything but your cock in my mouth." Drake leaned in and devoured Liam's mouth with a deep kiss.

Liam whimpered at the promise.

After they'd finished eating and some random movie was playing, Drake shoved the coffee table across the room and leaned against the couch before pulling Liam onto his lap to straddle him. Drake's hands gripped Liam's waist and his lips were rough and demanding on Liam's.

Liam rolled his hips, rocking their plump cocks together. He gripped the hem of Drake's shirt and pulled it over his head. Drake mirrored the action and soon their hot chests were plastered together as their mouths continued to nip, lick, and suck.

Drake's hands took hold of Liam's ass and kneaded gently. "This ass, so fine," he murmured.

"Thanks, I grew it myself," Liam teased and was rewarded with a deep chuckle from Drake.

"You grow this too?" Drake brushed his knuckles against Liam's zipper.

"Mmmhm."

"Strip. I wanna suck you," Drake demanded.

Liam stood, still straddling Drake's legs, and shucked his jeans and underwear.

Drake gripped the back of Liam's legs and pulled him forward.

Liam's legs bent slightly, knees on the couch straddling Drake's shoulders, and Liam's hands propped on the back of the couch. Drake gripped Liam's cock and stroked three times before opening his mouth and taking Liam deep. Drake's hands gripped Liam's hips and guided Liam's thrusts as he fucked in and out of Drake's mouth. Better than any movie they could have put on.

"You wanna come like this? Or with my cock buried in your ass?" Drake stroked Liam's dick as he spoke.

"Fuck me," Liam demanded.

Drake growled and pushed Liam away. "Bed?"

Liam couldn't help the lift of his brow. Drake asking for the bed seemed more intimate than the man usually wanted.

"More room." Drake shrugged. "I can take your ass right here on the floor if you want, but the carpet burn will be a bitch."

Liam rolled his eyes. "Bed is fine. You don't need an excuse." He headed down the hall, glancing over his shoulder to see Drake drop his pants and underwear before following him.

Drake met Liam at the edge of the bed in the dimly lit bedroom and captured his lips in a deep kiss. "I'm sorry I can't give more than this. But is this really all that bad?"

Liam's heart clenched. He wanted more. With Drake. And it was throwing his head and emotions for a loop. *Stop expecting more with him. Maybe you feel a connection, but he obviously doesn't. Yeah? Then why does he keep coming back to me?* Liam decided he would enjoy this while he could. In answer to Drake's question, Liam nibbled Drake's lip and whispered, "I'll take you whatever way I can get you."

Liam fell back on the bed and spread his legs, ready to take Drake.

Drake frowned. "Roll over, I want to see that pretty ass."

Liam's heart clenched again. Face down, ass up, less intimate than face-to-face fucking. But he longed for the invasion, the sting and stretch, the connection, so he moved to the middle of the bed and positioned himself on hands and knees.

Drake slapped his ass and licked a thumb before teasing his hole. "Look at that, love this ass."

"Fuck me, Drake. Get inside me, please," Liam begged.

"Patience. We're not rushing off to work this time. We've got more time. Let me play," Drake cooed and continued to tease Liam's ass. By the time Drake had worked three spit-slick fingers into his ass, Liam was squirming and whimpering while stroking his already primed to explode dick.

Drake paused. "Shit, condom's in my pants. You have one in here?"

Liam gestured wildly toward the bedside drawer.

Drake pulled out a condom and lube. With the wrapper torn open, latex rolled on, and lube spread, Drake hauled Liam's hips higher, lined up his cock at Liam's ass and pressed gently.

"Do it. Harder. Get in me." Liam slammed his hips back and groaned as Drake's cock sank deep.

Drake moaned. "God damn, so fuckin' tight." He set a hard and fast rhythm, his balls slapping Liam's, and fucked him good.

"Shit, fuck, so good," Liam chanted.

Drake thrust hard and deep, and Liam saw stars.

"Do that again," Liam demanded.

Drake gripped Liam's hips so tight Liam knew he'd feel the bruises for days. Drake fucked him deeply. "Jack yourself."

Liam took himself in his fist and stroked hard and fast.

With one final thrust, Drake roared and filled the condom, pulsing in Liam's ass as Liam shot his load all over his fist before Drake collapsed on him.

Several moments later, Drake pulled from Liam's ass gently. "Towel?"

"Bathroom," Liam grunted, unable and unwilling to move just yet.

Drake returned with a towel and tossed it at Liam's face.

Liam snorted and took a moment to clean himself up.

"Let's finish our food. I can't stay much longer," Drake said over his shoulder as he headed to the living room.

So much for cuddles and sleep Liam thought.

They sat in their underwear and finished their food. Even somewhat cold, pub food was delicious.

"So, no long luxurious talks cuddled in bed and waking up with each other," Liam ventured.

"What could we spend long luxurious moments talking about?"

"Work?" Liam suggested.

"I'll listen to your work stories if you want. My work stories are either confidential or beyond boring." Drake yawned. "And I can't spend the night. I'm a bed hog, plus I've got to be at work early. I need to get home and get to bed."

Liam pursed his lips and nodded. "I get it."

"Listen, it's all I've got to offer. I can't even say, *offer for now* because I don't see me ever being fit for a relationship. I'm married to my job. I've got issues. But, this? What we're doing? Casual, easy, good? I can do that. But I understand if it's not what you want." Drake stood and pulled on the rest of his clothes.

"No, what we're doing is good. It's fine. I want more, but I can be satisfied with this. For now."

Drake winced.

"What?"

"Nothing. Just the for now part."

Liam walked toward Drake and pulled him close. "Sorry, I'm not going to stop thinking it's for now. Maybe one day I'll wear you down and you'll realize that we could make it work."

"One day, you'll realize I'm not good for you and you'll move on. You'll find someone who can give you more than this. I'll be back to being a lonely, grumpy bastard. All will be right in the world." Drake kissed him. Hard.

But Liam turned the hard kiss into something softer, deeper, *more.*

Drake broke away with a ragged breath. "Tonight was great. We definitely need to do it again."

"We will," Liam promised. "Be safe going home." He watched as Drake descended the stairs and got in his car.

3
___

DRAKE

DRAKE READ over the detailed report one more time at his desk the next day. The body from the Shadow Woods apartment complex had been identified. Wade Bowers. Sixty-three, smoker, drinker, heart attack survivor. And a sex offender against juveniles. Drake clenched his jaw and swallowed the roiling bile.

Bowers was from the Indianapolis area. Drake had already found his last several known addresses and detailed reports citing his sexual crimes against children. A lot of children. He'd done a lot of time for several crimes, but was never locked up longer than a year or so at a time. Had a history of accusations made against him, but convictions not holding. Had a suspended sentence early on. Had a recent deferred sentence due to being the only caretaker available for his disabled brother. Bowers was one of those perpetrators who somehow always beat the system or slipped through cracks. Combination of dumb luck and a crappy system.

Wade had been drinking at the time of his death based

on the traces of alcohol found on his clothing—the report indicated alcohol was found in the body, but the decomposition had made it more difficult to trace. He was beaten and strangled before being buried in the cement.

Drake closed the file and leaned back in his desk chair before running both hands over his face. Wade Bowers was a monster, a pedophile, and a convicted sex offender.

But someone murdered him and that person broke the law.

Drake's job was to find the murder suspect, not get emotionally involved debating whether or not the victim deserved to die.

His phone buzzed.

Liam: Hey, I'm near the precinct. Want to grab lunch?

Drake looked at the time. Shit, how was it already lunchtime? He really shouldn't use up work hours chatting to Liam. But he did need to eat. The coffee and breakfast wrap had long worn off.

Drake: Sure. Can't take a long lunch, but I'll grab deli sandwiches and meet you at the park.

Liam: Okay. I want turkey, cheese, spinach, pickles, cucumbers, and spicy mustard. Thanks.

Drake: You have any waters? Bring some. I'm not buying drinks.

The three little dots appeared and disappeared enough times to lead Drake to believe Liam was likely struggling with whether or not to be a smartass. Liam always had an opinion and didn't usually hesitate to give it.

Liam: Bossy, cheap bastard. I'll bring waters.

Drake: You like when I'm bossy.

Liam: No argument there.

Fifteen minutes later, Drake plopped a deli bag on a

table under a shade tree in a picnic area not far from the precinct. A lot of employees took lunch and breaks there; Drake liked that it was close enough to buildings that smoking wasn't allowed.

Liam rolled his eyes. "Your tableside manners and presentation need a shit ton of work."

Drake snorted. "It's food, and you get my charming personality. Deal with it."

Liam chugged some of his water and Drake studied him.

Long-sleeve shirt, zippered hoody, worn jeans that fit Liam's ass like a damn glove, work boots, and a baseball cap. The man was fucking hot as hell. Any other guy would likely snap Liam up and never let him go.

Drake didn't have a choice. He'd enjoy the time he got with Liam. As long as he never let his feelings get involved, their eventual break-up wouldn't bother him in the least. Relationships were a lot like Drake's cases. The law made right and wrong clear. He didn't need emotions to solve a case, and he definitely didn't need his emotions involved with Liam. Emotions got a person in trouble. End of story.

Liam frowned as he sat down. "Penny for your thoughts?"

Drake grunted. "Just thinking about the body. Got the report that said who the victim was."

"Yeah? I'm guessing you can't give me details." Liam opened his sandwich and layered potato chips inside before closing it again and taking a huge bite.

"I mean, it's public knowledge by now. Pretty sure I saw it pop up on my news app." Drake bit into his meatball sub. "Wade Bowers. Sex offender from the Indy area."

Liam's eyes grew wide. "Damn, guess that makes your job easier."

Drake frowned. "How's that? I mean, we'll solve the case, but how's it easier?"

Liam shrugged. "Knowing it's some piece of shit child molester? I doubt I'd give another thought to figuring out who killed him."

Drake shook his head. "Doesn't work that way," he began, but his work phone buzzed. He stood after he read the text. "Damn it, Lieutenant Simms needs me back at the office."

Liam waved him off. "Go on. Thanks for lunch. We'll get together soon, yeah?"

Drake nodded as he gathered his trash and took another bite of his sandwich. He stalked away, phone in his right hand, sandwich in his left.

There was another damn body.

As Drake stalked toward Simms' office, Sam Mathers met him in the hallway.

"Drake," he said in way of a greeting and gave a nod of his head. "Heard you've got yourself another body. Feel free to hand over any unsolved cases; the Cold Case Unit could use some action."

"Fuck off, Mathers," Drake growled and fought the urge to roll his eyes as Sam fell into step beside him. "Got the I.D. on the most recent body, won't take long to land the suspect." He stopped and glared at Mathers. "And this new body will be no different. Sorry, man, you're going to have to go looking for action elsewhere."

"Speakin' of action," Mathers drawled and waggled his

brows. "How's the action in your life been lately? You getting' some?"

Drake stepped close enough to feel the heat from Mathers' body. "There's not a single detail of my sex life, hell, any damn part of my life, that's any of your damn business. So back the fuck off." Drake glared at Sam for a bit longer before grunting and walking away.

"Come on, Lewis, don't be like that. Just figured you've got them lined up waiting their turn. Probably can't keep up with them all. Any of the women you need to turn away or dump, feel free to send them my way." Sam clearly had no self-preservation skills and sucked at reading social cues because he continued to walk next to Drake and slapped him on the shoulder. "You can keep the guys, though. I'm fine with sloppy seconds of the female persuasion, but I don't bend the other way. Know what I mean?"

Drake sighed, glad he'd reached his destination. "Yeah, Mathers, I know what you mean. You're a horny bastard, a misogynistic pig, and a homophobic asshole. Got it." He didn't spare another breath to Sam Mathers before walking through the Simms' office door and slamming it behind him.

"Drake, glad you made it. Call came in about a body. Patrol reported first. Need you to get out there and see what's what." Drake's higher up, Lieutenant Simms, slapped him on the back. "I need you to check in on some of the new paperwork your team's been working on. Sign off on what you need to and then head to the address I'm going to send you."

Drake nodded. "Sounds good, thanks."

Simms went back to something at his desk and Drake left the office.

He had time to take a piss and grab a coffee, but his phone was buzzing with a text from the Lieutenant before Drake had time to stir in the sugar and cream.

The address made Drake frown as he slid into his car. He wasn't one hundred percent sure, but he'd almost place money that there was a construction project going on right around that same area. Another body? At another construction site? What were the odds?

Drake pulled up to the address and climbed from his car. As he walked toward the scene, he recognized several people.

But one person in particular.

"What the hell are you doing here?" Drake growled at Liam, low enough for no one else to hear. Hopefully.

"Chill, man," Liam whispered and glanced around to be sure no one was listening.

"Is this your site?" Drake demanded.

Liam gave a slight shake of his head. "Not mine. I mean, it belongs to our company, but I'm not the lead on this project."

"Then how the hell did you know to come here and why are you even here?" Drake didn't like Liam being connected to the crime in any way.

"Heard talk on the radios between the site crews. Bosses are moving guys from this site to some others for now so the men still get paid and other jobs can go ahead and be finished." Liam grimaced. "Second dead body at a second worksite isn't exactly good for productivity or business."

"So, your boss needed you here?" Drake crossed his

arms over his chest and tried to tamp down any hint of happiness at seeing Liam twice in one day.

Liam shrugged and smirked. "Figured you'd be here. Since we had to cut lunch short, I decided I'd come on over. Thought I'd come talk to the foreman of this site, buddy of mine, Bobby Castro. I bet he about shit himself to find a body on his site."

Drake scowled, that damn smirk of Liam's was as infuriating as it was intoxicating. "Well, tell the men to stay out of the way. Obviously, no one can cross the perimeter. At least this site isn't already up and running, no apartment dwellers constantly hanging around."

"Will do." Liam winked and looked around at the various crew members and police department people. "You think there's anything with the body being found at another one of our sites? Or just coincidence?"

Drake shrugged. "Don't know yet. Could go either way. But it wouldn't hurt to distance yourself from the scenes if possible."

Liam scrunched up his face. "Distance myself? Why? One, I'm the foreman of the first site. Two, I don't make a habit of killing people and burying them in wet cement."

Drake gave Liam a hard stare before pulling out his notebook to continue gathering information from those on the scene. He felt Liam's eyes on him, but Drake kept on working. And ignored the unfamiliar catch in his chest and the unwise desire to ask Liam if he wanted to get together that night. Drake crossed into the protected perimeter just to escape Liam's proximity. The man was making him think crazy things. Dates and relationship things. *Hell no. Get yourself together Lewis.*

An hour later, Liam appeared by Drake's side again.

"So, I talked with Bobby. He's shaken up. Said that concrete was just poured early this morning so it could be setting up before the crew arrived. Do you think the body was already there and the concrete truck driver didn't see it before he poured that basement wall? Or the driver poured the wall and *then* someone came and put the body in?" Liam asked, arms crossed on his chest, baseball cap pulled low as he stared over to the area where the body had been found. "I'm thinking the body was already in there. You could fit a decent sized person in the board forms of a wall setup like that." Liam whistled. "Damn, you think the body was already dead or did the killer put him in there alive and let him get smothered in concrete sludge? Those trucks are loud. If the victim was gagged, no one would have heard him over the sound of the truck."

Drake was slack-jawed and watching Liam with a curious stare. "That's a lot of questions and a lot of conjecture, Mr. Walters. And I already spoke to Bobby, but thanks for your input."

Liam shrugged. "This one is just more interesting than the one found at my site. This one couldn't have been here long. That form, all of the wall forms, have only been built and finalized within the last couple days. You think it was an air bubble or something that caused the form to buckle?" Liam scowled. "Seriously, if that form hadn't buckled, the crew wouldn't have taken the forms off for maybe a week. You think the body would have be completely hidden? Or visible?"

By that point, Drake realized Liam was just talking to himself mostly, as if he was trying to solve a television true crimes case. He shook his head. "I don't know. My job is to find out who did it, not entertain a thousand questions about what if and maybe." Drake winced inwardly. Actually, a thousand questions about what if and maybe added with gut instinct made up most of his job. But Liam's closeness had him completely off-kilter.

Liam blinked and came back to himself. "Sorry, just lots to wonder about." He glanced around "Hey, you want to come over for a while tonight? Pizza and beer?"

Drake's gut clenched. Why did he want so badly to say yes? It wasn't just the sex. Yes, the sex was amazing, but it hadn't been that long since he'd had himself balls deep in Liam's perfect ass. Drake wasn't desperate for a quick lay. So, why did he want to spend a quiet, comfortable evening at Liam's? Trouble, that's all it would be.

"Nah, man. Better pass this time," Drake replied and did his best not to notice the disappointment on Liam's face. "I'll be at the office late working on this new case and the other. Soon, though, yeah?"

Liam just nodded. "Sure." He gave a small wave and headed toward his truck.

THREE DAYS LATER, Drake was up to his elbows in paperwork and reports, questions and interviews, evidence and speculation. He ran a hand through his hair and closed his eyes.

Liam.

Every damn time Drake had closed his eyes lately, he'd seen Liam.

Liam's fine ass. His lean and muscular body. His lips, that smirk, those damn blue eyes.

"Fuck," Drake whispered.

He hadn't seen Liam for a few days. That wasn't a problem. In fact, it was probably for the best. Drake was busy. Liam was busy and needed to keep away from the cases and Drake.

So, why was Drake thinking about the man, wishing he would text him to have lunch, *missing* him?

"No, you don't miss him. It's just the stress of these two cases. Maybe plan a hookup soon, relieve some tension. That's all," Drake mumbled the words to himself, but even to his own ears they sounded weak, like a flimsy alibi.

A knock at the door brought Drake back to his senses.

Lieutenant Simms stood in the doorway. "Need you to go out, report of a body."

Drake huffed. "All due respect, sir, I'm kinda up to my neck in these two bodies already. Can't you send Spitz out?"

Simms shook his head, a scowl on his face. "Nah, need you. Seems like we've got ourselves a situation."

Drake raised a brow.

"Another body, another construction site, same company, buried in cement."

Drake ran a hand over his face. "Fuuuuck," he drawled.

4

———

LIAM

"Bobby, how's it going, man?" Liam asked his fellow foreman, Bobby Castro, as they watched the police crawl over the construction site. The moment a third body, the second at one of Castro's sites, showed up, Liam knew something major was going on. He'd heard the information on the news, not from Drake, which was disappointing. Liam knew that Drake couldn't share a lot of information. But once it hit the news and was open to the public, the least Drake could have done was contact him.

"Man, Walters, I gotta tell ya, I've been better," Bobby bit out and crushed a cigarette on the ground.

"Understandable."

"Like, so much shit's coming down from this. Losing time on the sites, moving men from my crews to others, police around all the time, everybody questioning and suspecting everyone." Bobby ran a hand over his face before lighting his second cigarette. "Hell, it's got me looking at every damn crew member, our outside contractors, everyone. When, in reality, it may not be anyone even related to the construction company. Maybe someone just seeing opportunity to dump some bodies." He drew in deep on the cigarette and blew the smoke out harshly. "But now my crew and production are going to shit and it looks bad against me."

Liam nodded. "It's odd that three bodies have shown up at Corsen Construction sites, two at yours. Feels like it *should* be someone with access to the sites, but, really, *anyone* could probably gain access if they waited for the right times." He shook his head. "Not really great for business being known as the company 'where all those bodies keep showing up buried in cement,'" Liam grumbled.

Liam and Bobby said their goodbyes and headed out to get done what work they could despite all the media and police presence in their daily jobs now.

By the end of what had proven to be an exhausting day, Liam dragged himself up the stairs and into his apartment. He wanted a shower, a beer, and bed. Maybe he'd cook up a microwave meal. He checked his phone thinking maybe Drake would have texted. But there was nothing.

"Get it together, Walters." Liam tossed his phone on the counter before running a hand through his work-messed hair. "You're nothing to him. A piece of ass. Maybe he enjoys time with you from time to time, but he's not the type to just text idle chatter."

Liam took a long, hot shower. The Drake of his steamy, wet fantasy was the type to talk, to care, to commit. And that thought nearly brought Liam to his knees as he gave his cock one final jerk.

He ended up heating up two hotdogs and eating Cheetos along with them while he zoned out in front of the television with a beer. By beer number two, Liam knew he might as well give up and go to bed; his eyes were heavy and he'd dozed off two or three times.

Cleaning up his late dinner first, Liam then brushed his teeth and crawled into bed. With one last look at his phone, which contained no messages from Drake, Liam fell into a fitful sleep.

He woke with a start. What had the noise been? Had he dreamed it? Liam's heart pounded in his chest when he heard the sound again and realized it was a knock at the door.

Rolling from bed, Liam grabbed a baseball bat from the closet. He'd never been comfortable around guns. Young Liam had seen guns used to threaten and control enough times that he didn't want to have them in his house since he wasn't properly trained, and he had no intention of getting gun training.

Surely a burglar wouldn't knock at the door.

But Liam didn't really have people who'd beat down his door at two-o'clock in the morning. He peeked through the peep-hole.

And froze.

He propped the baseball bat against the hall wall and unlocked the door.

Yanking the door open, Liam came face-to-face with the last person he ever expected to see on his doorstep.

Drake.

Drake looked to the ground, ran a hand over his face, then said, "I'm sorry," before stepping inside and pulling Liam into his arms.

Shocked, Liam didn't react at first, but then he pushed the door shut and melted into the hug.

They stood for what seemed like forever locked in each other's embrace.

Liam finally spoke, "Hey, not that I'm complaining. Not at all. But are you okay?"

Drake backed away from the hug a bit. "I'm sorry, I shouldn't have come here. It was stupid."

"No, don't apologize. I always want you to come to me." Liam kept his arms around Drake. "I was surprised, but not angry. I'm just concerned. Is everything okay?"

Drake kissed him, teasing Liam's lips until their tongues danced and Liam groaned.

"Can we talk after?" Drake growled.

Liam balked. "Is this just a booty call?" He frowned. He didn't want to discourage Drake's visits, but Liam wasn't sure he wanted to become the man's late night cum dump.

"No, I promise I'll talk and tell you why I'm here," Drake murmured. "I just need to hold you close and be with you."

"You'll talk? Cuddle? Stay?" Liam cocked a brow.

Drake nodded.

Liam kissed him, allowing their tongues to return to the thrusting and caressing of just moments before.

By the time the men had reached Liam's room, they were down to just their underwear.

Within twenty minutes, Drake had produced a condom and rolled it on, lubed himself and Liam's ass, plunged deep and hard into Liam's body, and spilled his release with a roar while Liam erupted in Drake's fist.

As they lay catching their breath, Drake mumbled, "Guess we should clean up so I can..." He paused.

Liam held his breath.

"Tell you what brought me to your door at two in the morning."

Liam released his breath. "Grab a towel."

Once they were cleaned up, Liam pulled down the blankets and laid on the left side of the bed while patting the right side for Drake. "Come on, get comfy."

Drake took a deep breath, and Liam felt somewhat bad that Drake was in an uncomfortable situation.

"Would you rather sit on the couch?"

Drake shook his head and climbed into the bed.

Liam pulled the covers over their bodies. He rolled to his side to face Drake.

Drake rolled so they were facing each other.

"Want me to ask questions? Or just start from the beginning?" Liam propped his head on his bent elbow.

"I think probably just let me talk," Drake whispered.

Liam nodded.

Drake took a deep breath. "I've never talked about my past. No clue why I think this is a good idea."

"You don't have to tell me anything you're not comfortable with. I'm just happy you didn't already skip out," Liam teased.

"My dad was an asshole. Is. My dad *is* an asshole," Drake began. "It's better now that I'm grown and don't have to deal with him daily. But growing up, he wasn't very kind. Ran the house with military precision. I think he truly loved my mom, but he wasn't an emotional or demonstrative man."

Liam raised a brow.

Drake gave a sardonic chuckle. "Yes, I recognize like father, like son." He frowned in the dimly lit room. "I don't want to be like him."

Liam stroked a hand down Drake's arm until he reached his hand. When Drake took hold of Liam's hand, it was unclear which of them was more shocked.

"This okay?" Liam held up their joined hands.

Drake nodded. "Anyway, my dad was a stickler for being on time, having a clean room, doing everything perfect. And if you didn't meet his expectations, you got the shit beat out of you. I mostly did everything he wanted. It was ingrained in me to follow the rules. Dad never saw gray, no in-between. With him it was always either black or white. And I grew up learning that. It serves me pretty well in my line of work."

He paused and absently stroked Liam's hand with his thumb.

"I watched my mom die."

Liam's breath caught. "I'm sorry."

"It was a robbery gone wrong. Maybe the robbers didn't expect us to be home. Maybe something else got fucked up. I don't know. I just know that I saw her shot, in a pool of her own blood on our living room floor, and all I could do was sit curled up in the corner of the couch until the police took me to the station. The officers took care of me; they made me feel less scared. Or as less scared as a kid can be when he's watched his mother die. They asked me questions and then got me a blanket and hot chocolate until my dad came to get me. Probably wasn't all that long, but to a young kid it felt like I was there for eternity. And I was so scared of how this was going to change things for my dad and me."

Liam scooched closer to Drake and cuddled against his chest.

"If my dad was strict and distant before, he became even more so after Mom died. Looking back, I think he just missed her terribly. But it sucked because he basically just existed. He didn't go to any of my school stuff. Didn't worry about fixing meals; I was old enough to fix my own food, but still. He barely spoke; he was a shell of the man he used to be. Dad never had a nice or encouraging word to say and I grew up convincing myself that emotions and love and all that good shit was just stuff in movies. I didn't need it, didn't want it. Or so I told myself."

They were quiet for several moments.

"So you heard about the third body?" Drake changed the subject.

Liam didn't mind, he wasn't sure his heart could take much more of Drake sharing about his past. "Yeah, it popped up on my news app. It's so crazy."

"You talk to Bobby Castro?"

"Yeah, went to see him today. He's a mess over everything."

"Gotta say, things don't look good for him," Drake stated.

"You think Bobby buried all those bodies?" Liam pulled back to frown at Drake.

Drake shrugged. "I'm not sure. But he'd have access to his own sites and the site where Wade Bowers was found."

"I would have had the same access. Do you think I killed those men?" Liam prodded.

"I'm so damn tired of bodies in concrete, bodies in general. I'm tired of working my ass off to solve one case only to have two more pop up." Drake sighed and ignored Liam's question. "I'm physically tired, mentally drained, and so damn worried I'll lose another case to the Cold Case Unit."

"You should try to sleep."

"I did try to sleep," Drake growled. "But the only damn thing I could think about was talking to you and holding you in my arms," Drake whispered. "And that scares the ever-loving fuck out of me."

Liam smiled slightly and allowed Drake's arms to clutch him tightly to his chest.

"We can be scared together," Liam whispered.

They fell asleep in each other's arms.

Liam woke a few hours later when Drake's cock nudged his hip. Based on the light coming in the windows, it was barely morning. Liam didn't often show up late to the jobsite, but for Drake, he'd make an exception. Would the man in his bed do the same?

Liam rolled so his back was to Drake, and groaned when Drake's hard length pressed against his ass.

Barely moving from Liam's side, Drake reached behind him to grab a condom and lube from the bedside table.

His slick fingers probed Liam's hole before his throbbing, hot cock pressed gently against his entrance. Drake lifted Liam's left leg as his dick invaded his body. The sting and stretch were exquisite, and Liam whimpered as Drake pumped in and out in a slow, gentle rhythm.

Drake kissed Liam's neck and whispered in his ear, "So damn tight and hot. So perfect. Nowhere else I'd rather be."

Those words were as close to a committed relationship

as Drake had ever gotten and they made Liam's cock pulse.

"I want to unload in your ass," Drake murmured. "Stroke yourself and come with me."

Liam gripped his own length and pumped hard in the same rhythm as Drake's cock thrusting into his ass. When his balls drew up tight, Liam knew he was a goner. He exploded all over his fist with a roar.

Drake rolled to his back, his cock still embedded in Liam's ass, and Liam laying on top of him. He took hold of both of Liam's hands and wrapped their arms around Liam's chest as he thrust slow and deep into his body. Drake's mouth was right at Liam's neck and he nipped, kissed, and suckled. "Fuck, Liam, I'm gonna blow."

"Do it, I want to feel it," Liam panted.

Drake moved their left arms down to pin Liam's waist as he thrust up one final time and moaned his release. Liam's ass clenched around Drake's pulsing cock as Drake held Liam tightly molded to his chest.

"Damn, never had anything better," Drake murmured. "Sex with you is like how you always *think* it's going to be with someone else, but then it never is. But with you, it's perfect and right every single time." He squeezed Liam's hands in his and rolled them to their sides. "You gotta work?"

Liam mumbled an affirmative. "But I can be late. What about you."

Drake chuckled. "Never been late a damn day in my life."

Liam started to get up.

"But I've got some time," he grumbled and pulled Liam close.

Sex with Drake, as he had already said, was always spectacular. But this morning had been different. Gentler? Maybe. There was something different between them and it had sparked the moment Liam opened the door and Drake hugged him.

"So tell me about your cases." Liam ran a hand over Drake's chest. "If you can."

"First body's been identified. Sixty-three, smoker, drinker, heart attack survivor. And a sex offender against juveniles." Drake's voice was tight. "From the Indy area. Several last known addresses. Slew of crimes against children."

"Fucker," Liam bit out. "Said it before and I'll say it again, damn piece of shit deserved it."

"Not my place to pass judgement, I just need to figure out who's killing people." Drake drew in a deep breath. "Second and third bodies haven't been identified yet. Both buried in concrete like the first one, but these two were somewhat better buried—maybe better thought out? And these two bodies were missing hands and other body parts. No finger prints. Have to ID another way."

"Ten-to-one says these other two are child sexual predators, too."

Drake pulled back. "Why would you say that?"

Liam shrugged. "Just a hunch. But if they are, they deserve it. No one will miss a damn child molester. Fuck, whoever did it should be thanked for clearing the streets of that trash."

"Hold up. You're getting way ahead of yourself. There's no proof that the other two guys are sexual predators. Could have been wrong place, wrong time. Or they owed money. Or got in with a bad crowd." Drake frowned. "And I hate what Wade Bowers did to children, but that doesn't excuse a murder. Two wrongs don't make a right. Whoever killed Wade and these other two guys, whether it's the same killer or different, needs to face consequences for taking a life."

"What consequences do sexual predators face?" Liam growled through clenched teeth. His heart thumped and his nostrils flared.

Drake's phone buzzed. "Damn, as—interesting?—as this conversation has been, I've got to get to work. Table it for now?"

Liam shrugged. "Yeah, just feel passionately about some things."

"I can't believe I'm going into work late because of a sleep over." Drake rubbed a hand over his face.

"I've been late a time or two, but never because of a man in my bed keeping me distracted." Liam leaned in and kissed Drake softly.

Thirty minutes later, Drake was gone and Liam was in his truck heading to a site. His phone buzzed.

Drake: *This is maybe the stupidest idea I've ever had.*

Liam: *???*

Drake: *It's only going to lead to trouble and hurt feelings.*

Liam: *What? I'm lost.*

Drake: *I've got a lake house. If you're interested, we could spend the weekend there.*

5

DRAKE

Never in his career had Drake taken an entire extended weekend off work. Yet after getting clearance from Simms and handing the cases over, *temporarily*, to his team and Spitz—the only other detective Drake would trust with the cases—there he was, parked in Liam's lot on a Thursday morning ready to spend four days with a man who had somehow, someway, become an important part of Drake's life. *When had that happened? Hell if Drake knew. One day he'd been avoiding relationships like the plague. The next he was thinking of Liam constantly and found himself wanting to spend time with Liam. While the sex was amazing, if Drake was being honest, it wasn't just the sex.*

He ran a hand over his face. His lieutenant was right. This little break would do him good. Let him clear his head. Anything he could be doing on the case at the moment was also doable by his trusted team and colleagues. Drake could work from the lake house if needed. Although Simms had been adamant that wouldn't be necessary. His lieutenant truly seemed to think Drake was well on his way to a breakdown.

Drake texted Liam. *I'm here. Need help carrying anything?*

The apartment door swung open and Liam appeared with a duffle swung over his shoulder.

Drake couldn't keep his eyes off Liam as the man walked down the stairs.

"Hey." Liam tossed his bag in the backseat.

"Hey," Drake whispered gruffly in Liam's ear as he leaned in to kiss him.

"Someone may see," Liam warned.

Drake grunted and put the car into gear. "You want to stop for coffee?"

"God, yes."

Drake drove south on I-65 for about ten minutes and took the Main Street exit in Greenwood. "Starbucks okay?"

Liam nodded with a smile.

"Drive-thru or inside?" Drake turned on his turn signal for the left turn into the coffee shop.

"Drive-thru. I'm ready to hit the road." Liam wiggled in his seat like a small child.

Drake laughed.

Once Liam had his drink and scones, and Drake had his own beverage and a breakfast sandwich, they were ready to head out again.

Drake directed the car west on Main Street. "We'll just cut through town to 37."

"Where is this lake house?" Liam asked. "And might I add how shocked I am that you have a lake house?"

Drake snorted. "Why?"

It was Liam's turn to snort. "Lake houses seem

peaceful and relaxing. You don't seem like you've relaxed a single day in your life."

Drake shrugged, the comment a little closer to home than he cared to admit. "It's down in Brown County. We'll stop at Oliver Winery on the way; have a tasting and lunch. If you want?" He spared a glance Liam's way. When Liam nodded, Drake continued. "The house was my dad's. He was going to sell it, so I bought it from him. I keep it maintained. By *I*, I mean I pay someone to keep it clean and do the upkeep. I've thought about renting it out like an AirBnB thing. We'll be close enough we could drive into town if we need or want anything. There's good food and shops. But we'll have everything we need at the house so we don't *have* to leave."

Liam finished his last scone and brushed crumbs into his hand to toss them out the window. "You go to the lake often?"

Drake gave him a look. "This is the first time in my entire career that I've taken off more than one day at a time."

"So, I'm guessing that's a no?" Liam teased.

"You'd be correct."

"Was it hard to get the time off?"

Drake shook his head. "No. I've never taken a lot of time, so I've got it saved. Lieutenant is concerned about my mental health over these three cases. I think he's convinced I'm going to have a stroke." Drake chuckled. "Since we have a possible serial killer, the cases may get a lot more coverage from the state soon. Maybe even federal. Simms nearly made me sign in blood when I mentioned a break at the lake house sounded good. I was only partially serious, but he thought it would be beneficial to step back from the cases and gather my thoughts. Maybe if I worked for the state or the feds, I couldn't take days like this, but I'm lucky my higher ups trust me and give me freedom to work the cases as I see fit. And since Simms basically packed my bags for me, I don't really have a choice."

"Is it going to be hard to be off for four whole days?" Liam turned in his seat to face Drake more fully.

"I left my work that *can* be done by others to my most trusted colleagues. There's one other detective in my department whom I trust. Spitz is taking over the cases for the weekend. I can work from the lake house if needed."

"How many times have you practiced saying that?" Liam smirked when Drake glanced his way.

"If I keep saying it, maybe I'll eventually believe it. All I'm missing is pouring over security camera footage, interviewing possible witnesses, and snatching up any information the lab can provide. Things don't happen as quickly in real life as they do on television."

"Why this weekend? Why the lake house? Why me?" Liam's questions poured from him and took Drake by surprise. "Don't get me wrong. I love that we're together, taking a little getaway, but I just wondered what changed."

Drake chewed the inside of his cheek for a few moments. "Not really sure I can explain it."

Liam sighed. "Maybe sometime this weekend?"

Drake nodded. "If I can figure out how to put it in words."

About forty minutes of comfortable conversation later, Drake took a left turn from southbound 37 and wound around until he reached the parking lot of Oliver Winery.

"You been here?" Drake asked Liam as they climbed from the vehicle.

"Maybe once? I've had their wine, it's good. I think I came down here a few years ago. Or maybe I've only driven by it on the way to football games?" Liam scrunched up his face as he studied the winery's main building.

They walked through the pathway toward the building. Spring flowers were beginning to bloom and the sun was bright despite the cool breeze.

"The patio area is really nice on a warmer day. We can do our tasting and then eat lunch outside if you don't think it's too cool." Drake opened the door for Liam as he felt his phone buzz. He pulled it from his pocket and frowned.

"Work?" Liam guessed.

"Yeah, but it can wait."

Liam pulled a mock scowl. "Who are you and what have you done with Drake Lewis?"

Drake laughed. "It's not an emergency. I'll reply in a bit."

"No new body?"

"Thank God, no."

"Do you ever worry that a suspect will target you because of your work on a case? Or target your friends or family?" Liam frowned.

Drake shrugged. "I don't dwell on it. But if the murderer is aware of me working his case, escaping to the lake house is a perfect plan." He smiled and attempted to derail Liam's concerns.

Thirty minutes later, Drake and Liam took a bottle of sweet red along with a tray of meats, cheeses, and crackers to the heated patio. "Ah, they've got it nice and warm out here. I'm ready for the air to warm up."

Liam opened the wine while Drake spread out the food.

"I can't believe we like the same wine. I figured we'd be complete opposites." Liam poured two glasses.

Drake shrugged. "I can't help it. Sweet is the only wine I like."

"I hear ya. I hate having to defend my wine preference. Some people are so snobbish about it. Like dry is the *only* type of wine you can drink if you're a *real* wine drinker." Liam took a seat.

"Yeah, I'd rather actually enjoy what I'm drinking than try to prove something." Drake picked up his glass. "To a relaxing weekend."

"A relaxing weekend." Liam clinked his glass. "And to you solving your cases."

"Yes, please."

When their wine and food were gone, Drake began to clear the table. "You want to take some wine with us?"

"Sounds good. And chocolate. I need chocolate." Liam licked his lips.

Drake groaned. "Don't do things like that. It makes me want to jump you and that doesn't seem winery patio appropriate."

Liam laughed and gathered their empty bottle and glasses.

Twenty minutes later, Drake and Liam headed to the parking lot with six wines and assorted chocolates.

"I can't believe we bought six wines."

"What? The more you buy, the better the discount. If we don't drink them all this weekend, we'll leave them for the next time." Drake popped the trunk to store the box and then realized what he'd said. "If I rent the house out, the wine could be a gift for the guests." He stumbled through the flimsy excuse as his heart beat in his chest. When had he started including Liam in his future plans?

Liam smirked. "Good plan."

Drake maneuvered the car back to the highway. "I was thinking we'd stop for groceries. That way we don't *have* to get out if we don't want to."

"Plan on keeping me tied up and unpresentable all weekend?" Liam waggled his brows.

Drake's cheeks heated. "Just thinking ahead. Better to have food on hand in case we don't want to go out."

Liam swatted at Drake's arm. "You know I'm just giving you a hard time, right?"

Drake didn't even think, he grabbed Liam's hand and entwined their fingers. "I can take it." His heart fluttered and he glared at their connected hands.

"You okay? You look pissed." Liam gave Drake a questioning concerned look.

Drake shook his head, breaking free from staring at their hands. "Yeah, just...um, just never been the type for hand holding."

"You don't have to," Liam started.

"No, I want to." Drake cleared his throat. "I think that's why I'm a little off-kilter. Never *wanted* to hold a guy's hand."

"I guess I'll take that as a compliment." Liam winked.

By the time Drake pulled into a small local grocery store, he'd decided Liam's hand in his was *right* and *perfect* and he never wanted to let go. Holy hell, what the actual fuck was going on with him? It was like he'd lost his damn mind over the cases and now he was acting like a completely different person. Not that enjoying time with Liam was *bad*, it was just totally new to Drake and had him feeling confused.

Liam grabbed a cart as they entered the tiny store. "Where do you want to start?"

"Cold stuff last, of course."

Liam scoffed. "Of course. I should have known you'd have a plan of attack for grocery shopping."

Drake frowned. "Just makes sense. Cold stuff last so it doesn't get warm in the cart." He directed the cart toward the first aisle. "Pick a cereal." Drake chose a bran cereal with raisins.

Liam picked up a sugary, cinnamon cereal.

"Such a child," Drake murmured in Liam's ear and rubbed his front against Liam's back.

"Such a bore," Liam retorted and bumped his ass into Drake's groin. "Bran cereal?"

"Fiber is good for you. And it's not boring, it's got raisins." Drake attempted to be offended.

"Oh, raisins! Yes, raisins are *so* exciting." Liam snickered. His laugh stopped short when Drake nuzzled Liam's neck.

"Let's hurry this up. I'm suddenly ready to get to the lake house." Drake nudged the cart. "Soups? Dry goods?"

They spent the next ten minutes gathering foods that would be good to have on hand.

"Can always keep what we don't need for the renters," Liam suggested.

Drake narrowed his eyes. "Yeah. Or the next time we come down."

Liam's "mhmm" made Drake smile slyly.

The dairy and meats areas were last, and they eventually made their way to the checkout.

Once the car was loaded, Drake traveled a bit on the main drag before taking a smaller side road which led to a dusty gravel road that bordered a wide sparkling lake.

"Wow, is that *the* lake of the lake house?" Liam's gaze was directed out the window.

"Yep, few more twists and turns and we'll be there."

When Drake slowed the car, Liam glanced out the windshield. "Holy shit. You said lake house. This is more like a lake mansion."

"Nah, it's big but it's not super fancy." Drake killed the engine and popped the trunk. "I hope it's clean. The crew was supposed to be here this past weekend."

Drake hefted luggage and grocery bags and waited for Liam to do the same. He turned to study the lake house he'd only stayed at a few times when he was younger. The view from the driveway was impressive, but Drake knew the real beauty was on the backside of the house.

The groceries were put away first.

"Can I get a tour?" Liam glanced around the large, spacious kitchen.

"Sure." Drake grabbed his own duffle. "There's a master and two guest rooms. You're welcome to any of them."

Liam's face fell. "I mean, I guess a guest room is fine if that's where you want me."

Drake dropped his bag and stalked toward Liam. When he reached him, Drake pushed Liam back, back, back until they were stopped by the kitchen counter. "Where I want you is in my arms, in my bed, under me, around me." Drake's mouth devoured Liam's for several moments before they broke for air. "I was trying to be gentlemanly. I didn't want you thinking I only invited you here for sex."

"I didn't think you did. Although, I'm not going to complain about four days of sex." Liam nibbled at Drake's jaw. "Ready to tell me why you *did* bring me here?"

Drake groaned. "Not yet."

Liam pursed his lips. "Fine. I want a tour. Maybe you can tell me later."

"Maybe." Drake had a jumble of words and thoughts in his head. He wanted to lay them all out and try to make sense of them, but he wasn't sure he could do them justice.

"Stop overthinking things." Liam patted his cheek. "Show me around."

Ten minutes later they stood on the private dock and looked back at the house. Sunlight glinted off the arched windows, a squirrel paused on the wooden steps to nibble an acorn, and frogs croaked at the shallow lake edge.

"This is quite possibly one of the most beautiful places I've ever been." Liam turned in a circle. "You could definitely rent this out for a pretty penny. Private dock, firepit, grilling area, deck, gorgeous inside, picturesque outside. Fall on an Indiana lake? Doesn't get much better. You'd likely be booked solid at all times, but Fall would make a killing. For real."

Drake nodded. "Yeah. Thought about getting a pontoon boat, too. But then there's liability issues. Would have to look into that more." He put an arm around Liam. "It really is a great area."

"We should grill out tonight. Eat by the fire."

"Good plan. What do you want to do between now and dinner?"

Liam turned in Drake's arms. He nibbled on his own lip and blushed. "I'm thinking you could give me a tour of the house."

Drake raised a brow.

"Starting with the master bedroom."

Drake smirked.

"Specifically the *bed* in the master bedroom." Liam's cinnamon-scented breath brushed against the corner of Drake's lips.

"That can definitely be arranged." Drake captured Liam's mouth and kissed him deeply.

After coming up for air, Liam grabbed Drake's hand and led him up the steps from the dock to the house. They all but fell into the house in a knot of arms and lips and tongues. Shoes, shirts, and pants were discarded as they made their way up the stairs.

Drake maneuvered Liam into the sunlit master bedroom and pressed him against the navy and maroon bedspread until Liam fell backwards pulling Drake with him.

Drake grunted as Liam opened his legs to make room for Drake's hips. His cock strained against his boxer briefs. Drake pulled back just long enough to strip his boxers and yank Liam's off as well. He moved their bodies into the classic *sixty-nine* position.

"Fuck my face," Drake commanded.

"My pleasure, but only if you do the same." Liam licked Drake's slit.

Cocks thrust, tongues licked, and mouths sucked until

Liam gasped and pulled away. "Stop. I need you in my ass."

Drake growled and rolled to his back, yanked open a drawer, and fished around for a condom and lube, glad he'd thrown them in there earlier. "Ride me." He ripped the package open, rolled the condom down his length, and smeared lube on his cock.

Liam straddled Drake's hips and reached back to guide the man's cock to his hole. Drake thrust into Liam's ass slowly, loving the tight heat.

Without warning, Drake rolled them until Liam was flat on his back.

"What's wrong?"

"Just want to see my cock in your ass." Drake pressed in deep.

Liam groaned. "Fuck, yes."

Drake thrust in hard and moaned when Liam wrapped his legs around Drake's waist. "You feel so fuckin' good, baby." For a split second, Drake thought to cringe at the endearing word he'd *never* used before, but Liam's ass clenched around Drake's cock and all thought was lost. "Jack yourself."

Liam gripped his own cock as Drake pounded into his ass.

"Drake, I'm not gonna last. Gonna come."

"Come for me," Drake demanded.

Liam jerked and shot his load between them as Drake's cock unloaded, pulsing in Liam's ass.

"Jesus, that was hot." Liam panted under Drake.

Drake couldn't move, could only hold Liam close as their bodies shook from their orgasms.

A few minutes later, Liam groaned. "This is amazing, but my leg is getting a cramp."

Drake chuckled and pulled out before rolling to his side and removing the condom. A quick trip to the bathroom provided a towel for clean-up before Drake was back in bed within moments and pulled Liam close.

"So, about this weekend," Drake began gruffly.

Liam cocked a brow. "Yeah?"

"I'm married to my job. I have no time for relationships. I don't do commitment."

"Gee, don't oversell yourself," Liam scoffed.

"Shut up, just let me talk." Drake ran a hand up and down Liam's arm. "I've always been perfectly fine with quick and easy hookups, no strings, no expectations."

Liam started to speak, but Drake gave him a look to shut him up.

"Sorry. Please continue."

"And that was all I thought this thing with you was. We met. The sex was great. End of story. I was perfectly happy with a few more casual hookups after we met again at the construction site."

"But?"

Drake ran a hand over his face. "But…hell, I don't even know. Somewhere along the line, maybe somewhere between the stress of body two and body three, I found myself thinking about you as more than a casual fling. You somehow became the first thing I thought of when I woke up, and the last thing before I go to sleep. When the stress and frustration of the job is getting to me, it's you I want to talk to. Hell, I want to share my stories with you."

Liam was silent and Drake worried he'd gone too far.

But Liam's bright eyes gave Drake hope.

"I'm sorry, I know you came into this thinking it was completely casual. And that's what it was meant to be."

Liam smiled and kissed Drake. "I'm not upset. I've made it clear I was comfortable with what we had for the time being, but that I'm also interested in more. I would be completely fine with us making whatever this is more serious, more committed."

Drake's heart flopped in his chest. "Damn, I didn't realize how worried I was that you wouldn't want the same." He kissed a smiling Liam. "I'm a bitch when I'm in the middle of cases. Which is almost always. I work too much. I work too late. I let the case consume me."

"Would you say that the time we've spent together from the first body until the moment you picked me up for this weekend is normal work behavior for you?" Liam shifted a leg and pressed his knee between Drake's legs.

Drake took the question seriously for a moment before replying, "I'd say it's slightly above average as far as how much I've been working, how stressed I've been, and how consumed I've been by the cases. Why?"

Liam smiled and caressed his hand along the curve of Drake's hip. "We've spent time together during that time period. Gone out, had dinner, enjoyed each other's company. I'm comfortable with what we've had. I think we could easily make it work. It's not like I'll be home pining away for you at all times. My hours can get wonky, and I'm usually exhausted when I get home."

"I've always thought that bringing another person into my life would just be asking for trouble." Drake sighed. "But the thought of not having you stresses me out more than these damn dead bodies."

"So, what does that mean?" Liam bit his lip. "Exclusive?"

"Hell yes, exclusive. I'm not sharing."

"Boyfriends?" Liam prodded.

Drake's eyes went wide and he felt the need to protest. But he whispered the word as if tasting it, testing it. "Boyfriends?" Drake's face softened with a smile. "Boyfriends." This time he said the word more as a statement than a question. "I can't believe I'm saying this, but I like the sound of that." He pulled Liam close. "I think maybe I need to show my *boyfriend* just how much I like the sound of that."

Liam rolled to his back and spread his legs. "I think that's an amazing idea."

"As soon as possible, I want us both tested so we can do this without condoms. You okay with that?" Drake spoke as he rolled the latex down his length.

Liam's breath caught in his throat. "God, yes."

Drake pressed his cock against Liam's pucker and inched his way in slowly.

Liam moaned. "Slow, I'm kinda sore."

"Need to stop?"

"No, just go slow."

Moments later, Drake had set such a maddeningly slow pace that Liam was begging for him to go faster.

"Please, Drake. Faster, harder." Liam attempted to pull Drake in deeper with his legs.

"Mmm, no. Don't want to hurt you. Gotta go slow." Drake kissed Liam's neck before capturing his mouth. He continued the slow rhythm, but increased the power behind his thrusts.

Drake maneuvered their bodies to the edge of the bed

so he could stand as he fucked into Liam's body. He gripped Liam's cock and stroked in the same crazy slow rhythm.

"Please, Drake." Liam planted his feet and fucked his ass on Drake's cock until Drake broke and sped up his thrusts. "Oh God, yes. Harder, faster."

Drake growled. "You damn bossy bottom." But he pumped into Liam's ass in powerful thrusts until his balls drew up. "Come with me."

Liam groaned as he spilled himself over Drake's fist.

Drake stilled and shot deep in Liam's ass.

"Boyfriend sex is even better than no commitment, no expectations sex." Drake's words were muffled against Liam's neck.

"Agreed," Liam panted. "So, are you keeping me in bed all weekend?"

"Sounds like an amazing plan."

Liam smacked Drake's ass.

"Fine, fine. I guess we can get out of bed from time to time." Drake rolled from Liam's body. "I was thinking we'd take a boat out. Maybe sleep under the stars one night? Go hiking?"

"That sounds amazing," Liam murmured.

After a quick shower, Drake pulled Liam into his arms and covered them with the blanket before they fell asleep.

6

LIAM

THE NEXT MORNING, Drake and Liam sat outside on the deck watching the sun rise over the lake while they sipped coffee.

"You know your concrete guy very well?" Drake asked. The question came out of the blue.

"Dave Houston?" Liam eyed Drake over his mug. "I've worked with him for quite a while. Why?"

Drake's brows drew into a scowl. "In talking to crew members, Dave's name has come up a lot. Couple guys mentioned how Dave had started coming in super early a couple days a week, taking the concrete truck out to sites a lot earlier than is usual. Leaving other jobs to the rest of the crew."

It was Liam's turn to frown. "You're thinking *Dave* might be a suspect?"

Drake shrugged. "Changes in behavior, access to sites, can't say he's not looking somewhat suspicious."

"Pretty sure he's got a new baby at home. Things

change." Liam plunked down his coffee cup on the table. "Dave doesn't seem like the murdering type."

Drake scoffed. "Neither did Ted Bundy, John Wayne Gacy, or Gary Ridgeway. A lot of killers don't *seem* like the murdering type."

"Well, let's see then. According to you, *I* could be the murderer since I don't fit the type and also have access to the sites. Looks bad for Bobby Castro. Now it looks bad for Dave Houston. You have any suspects outside of my company?" Liam crossed his arms over his chest.

Drake drew in a long breath. "Sorry, I promised to try not to work this weekend. Houston's just been niggling at me for a while." He drained his coffee. "You want to hike first or take the boat out?"

Liam frowned, not completely ready to let go of the discussion, but realized it was likely for the best. He took one last swig of coffee, pushed aside his irritation, and opted for a hike first. They changed clothes before heading out.

"I need a stick." Liam glanced around at the wooded area fifteen minutes later. "I can't hike without a stick."

"I'll give you a stick," Drake's rumbly voice teased at Liam's ear as he rubbed his dick against Liam's ass.

"Perv. Hiking is not sexy time. Sexy time during hiking ends up with bug bites and poison ivy. Behave." Liam spotted the perfect walking stick and held it up with a triumphant grin. "Yes! Now we can hike."

"But I don't have a stick." Drake pouted adorably.

"We'll find you one, let's go." Liam headed down the path.

"We couldn't hike without *you* having a stick, but it's

fine for me to hike without one? How's that fair?" Drake put his hands on his hips.

"You only want a stick because I have one. We'll get you one, but it wasn't a *need* for you. It's just a want. So, we can start walking and find you one on the way."

Drake rolled his eyes but he laughed.

About five minutes into their hike, Liam grabbed a stick. "Here, this is a good one."

Drake tested it out. "Very nice. Now the real hiking can begin, right?"

Liam nodded. "We are now explorers, voyagers, adventurers. Keep your eyes open for wild animals and danger."

Drake chuckled. "We're in Brown County, Indiana. I don't think there's much danger."

"You never know when the wild animals may take umbrage with us being in their natural habitat and attack." Liam strained to keep a straight face.

"Umbrage? Can wild animals take umbrage?" Drake narrowed his eyes.

"Best to be prepared." Liam winked before finally cracking a smile.

Two hours later, they'd observed several deer, about ten turtles sunning on a log at the lake edge, a momma duck and her babies rushing into the water, and a large black snake warming itself in the sun at the edge of the woods. No umbrage had been taken, and no attacks had been launched.

"Shit, I'm exhausted." Liam drained a fourth bottle of water as they exited the wooded area near the house.

Drake did the same. "Me too. You want to do the boat or a nap?"

Liam thought it over. "Let's get more water and some food. We could sleep on the boat, right?"

Drake nodded with a smile. "Yep, I was going to borrow the neighbor's pontoon boat. We'll go to a quiet little cove and anchor down. Lunch and a nap on the water sounds amazing."

They grabbed a picnic cooler and some blankets and pillows from the house. Drake texted the neighbor to secure permission and then tromped down to the neighboring dock.

"How'd you learn to drive a boat?" Liam frowned. "Is it called *driving* a boat?"

"Pilot, steer, sail, among others." Drake maneuvered the pontoon boat away from the dock. "My dad taught me. We didn't do a lot after Mom died, but he made sure I knew my way around a water craft." The boat idled for a bit before Drake pointed them toward the cove. "There's this great little spot around the bend. It's super quiet and private. Great spot to just sit and relax. I remember Dad bringing me here after Mom died. The last time we were here, we sat for hours in the cove. I think Dad was lost in his grief and pretty much forgot I was there."

Liam wrapped his arms around Drake. "That had to suck."

Drake shrugged. "Kinda. But I enjoyed watching the animals. Lots to see on the banks, in the water, and in the air."

They stood silently for a moment.

Drake pointed to the sky. "Watch that bird."

The bird torpedoed toward the water and snatched a fish.

"Whoa," Liam exclaimed. "Pretty cool."

"You want to grab lunch?" Drake kept his hands on Liam's arms still wrapped around his waist.

Liam's stomach grumbled in answer. "That would be a yes."

Drake moved the cooler toward the bench seat and spread a blanket on the floor of the boat. He placed sandwiches, grapes, chips, and drinks on the blanket before plopping down and leaning his back against the bench. He patted the spot next to him.

Liam smiled and joined him on the blanket. "Can I ask you something?"

"You just did."

"Smart ass." Liam bumped Drake's shoulder. "What's changed? When we've been together in the city, you're always aloof, removed, never wanting anyone to think you're on a date or *with* me."

Drake reached for Liam's hand, but let the man keep speaking.

"But out here, you're so much more open, relaxed, dare I say *romantic*." Liam squeezed Drake's hand. "Don't get me wrong. I'm not complaining. I love this. But it's a little frustrating to be *hidden* in the city." *Like you won't even come to my door to pick me up*, Liam thought to himself.

Drake took a deep breath. "I'm working on that. Definitely."

Liam took a bite of a sandwich and chewed until Drake continued.

"I've never lied about who I am, but after being on the force for so many years I've never figured out a way to bring up the fact that I'm gay." Drake popped a chip in his mouth. "I go out, but stick to the gay friendly areas if I'm with a guy. Figure there's less chance seeing anyone I work with, and if I see anyone I work with they'll likely be doing the same thing as me."

"Sounds exhausting." Liam hated thinking of Drake hiding and not able to be himself. Selfishly, he wanted Drake to be proud of them being out on the town together.

Drake pursed his lips together and shrugged. "Not too bad because I never really do much socializing. I may meet up here and there, hook up from time to time, but I don't go out much. Grab food from the pub. Maybe some drinks alone at a bar."

Liam took the last bite of his sandwich, finished chewing, and said, "Until me." His heart flip-flopped.

Drake nodded. "Until you." He chuckled. "Yeah, you threw a wrench in my plans for sure. You weren't supposed to be more than a one-time thing. I liked you, sex was great, but I wasn't looking for anything more."

"But?"

"But the universe must have laughed its ass off when I made that plan because it brought you back into my life and made me realize that things were much better when I had you around." Drake lifted his eyes to meet Liam's. "Despite how much I tried to avoid it."

Liam moved quickly to straddle Drake's hips and wrapped his arms around Drake's neck. "Sorry to mess up your plans."

"Apology not accepted because I'm not sorry you messed up my plans."

"Good because I'm not *really* sorry." Liam rolled his ass on Drake's lap.

Drake snaked an arm up and around Liam's neck and pulled him close for a kiss.

When they were both out of breath, Drake broke the kiss and left Liam panting. "I can't promise I'll work less. I can't promise I'll announce I'm gay at work. But I can promise that I'll do less hiding, be more open about who I am, even if that means the department finding out."

Liam frowned. "Do you think it could affect your job? I wouldn't want that."

Drake shrugged. "Vast majority wouldn't care. Maybe some even already know or at least suspect. I can think of a handful who would have a problem with it. But none of them could do anything to my position on the force. The only way my job is affected is if I screw up, break rules, that type thing."

Liam moved from Drake's lap and stretched out on the blanket pulling Drake with him. "That's good to hear. How can a boat make me so damn sleepy?"

Drake nuzzled Liam's neck. "It's the movement, like rocking a baby. Sleep." He put a pillow under Liam's head and snuggled close to share it.

Sometime later, Liam slowly came to from a luxurious nap and realized he was curled in Drake's arms on the floor of the boat. He also realized that Drake didn't seem to give a damn if any passers-by on the lake saw them cuddled together. Liam decided he'd be completely happy to wake up in Drake's arms every day. Damn, how things had changed. Mr. Unattached, King of No Commitments, Prince Hook-Up was Liam's *boyfriend* and it didn't seem to be freaking Drake out in the slightest.

Drake stirred and moaned.

"Can we nap on the lake every day?" Liam mumbled into Drake's chest.

"Maybe not every day." Drake tightened his arms

around Liam. "But every time we're at the lake house, for sure."

"Deal."

"You want to head back? Shower? Dinner outside?"

"Think we could camp out?" Liam sat up.

"Not a full-blown camp out, don't have the supplies." Drake stood and pulled Liam to his feet. "But I was thinking a totally primitive blanket under the stars; curl up in a sleeping bag if it gets too cool."

"Not sure that's *totally primitive*, but it sounds amazing. What should we do for dinner?"

"Hot dogs over an open fire?" Drake lifted a brow.

"Mmmm, yes. Sounds amazing. That's one thing about living in the city, can't really do the whole wiener roast thing too easily."

Drake steered the boat back to his neighbor's dock and tied it off.

"You know your neighbors?" Liam nodded toward the neighboring home up the hill.

"Not super close, but yeah, I know them. Nice folks. Retired from the city. Live here full time now. Kids are grown. Their grandkids come over a lot. Paul and Carol, the ones who live there, they keep an eye on the house for me. They check in on me through text from time-to-time, let me know if a limb is down or if the cleaning crew showed up."

"Nice that they let you borrow their boat," Liam said as the two men climbed the steps to the house.

"Shower?" Drake asked.

"As in shower and be done or are we making this an event?" Liam cocked his head.

Drake chuckled. "As much as I could get into a double

shower, I'm thinking we'd get more fireside time, hotdog time, and under the stars time if we take separate showers."

"Agreed." Liam kissed Drake. "But tomorrow morning, I say double shower is needed."

"Deal."

After separate showers, Drake and Liam packed up food, drinks, and snacks. Drake pulled out two blankets, two pillows, and a rolled-up sleeping bag.

"We'll have light for another couple hours, but the sun will set a lot earlier right now. By summer, we'll have light past ten o'clock." Drake set up a small table for the food while Liam unfolded chairs.

Liam's heart warmed when he thought of coming back to the lake during the summer. "Beer or wine before dinner?" He held up a can of beer in one hand and a bottle of wine in the other.

Drake piled up logs for the fire. "Beer now. Wine as an after-dinner treat." He winked.

An hour later, the fire crackled and Liam groaned. "Oh my God, I should have stopped with two hotdogs. A third was just ridiculous. But they were so good."

"Nothing like a fire roasted hotdog." Drake poured two glasses of the sweet red wine. "Come on, let's lie down."

By the time the men were situated on the blanket, the warmth of the fire at their backs, wine in hand, Liam noted the sun was beginning its slow descent on the horizon. The sky glowed in vibrant oranges, pinks, and soft blues.

For over an hour, Drake and Liam sipped wine, listened to an insect serenade, watched the blazing sun slip behind the lake, and talked about anything and everything as the fire crackled behind them.

"Fireflies will be pretty out here over the summer," Drake mused.

"Definitely. I love the sounds the frogs make, too." Liam set his glass to the side and moved so he was flat on the blanket, arm behind his head. "It's amazing how bright the stars seem out here away from all the city lights."

Drake moved into the same position. "Yeah, the light pollution in and around the city is crazy." He reached for Liam's hand. "Do you know the constellations?"

"Nah. I'm sure I learned some of them in school, but they never stuck. You?" Liam caressed Drake's hand with his thumb.

"Not really. I can find the Big Dipper and Little Dipper. Maybe Orion's Belt. Which one has the North Star?" Drake mused.

"Hell if I know. I'm lucky to find the damn moon." Liam wiggled closer to Drake loving the warmth of Drake's body next to his own.

"If our reception out here was better, we could look it up." Drake picked up his phone but almost immediately tossed it down.

"Or just enjoy the stars."

"Holy shit, did you see that?" Drake pushed up onto his elbow. "Was that a shooting star?"

Liam sat up. "I didn't see it. I've never seen more than one or two and even then I wasn't sure they were really shooting stars."

"Look, there's another one!" Drake pointed.

"Damn it, I missed it again." Liam frowned. "I wonder

if there's some sort of meteor shower tonight. Now I need to see one, I can't let you win." Liam laid back down on his back, propping his head on his arms.

Drake laughed and ran a hand up Liam's stomach before leaning in close.

"No kissing," Liam admonished. "I need to see a shooting star."

"What if you don't?" Drake rubbed his hand on Liam's chest.

"No sex until I see a damn shooting star."

Drake groaned but returned to his back to watch the night sky. "You're kinda a brat, you know that?"

"How's that?" Liam asked but didn't look Drake's way.

"Just sort of seem to be used to getting your way."

Liam hummed. "Maybe. But you got to see two shooting stars. I want to see one. Then we can play."

Ten minutes later, Drake huffed. "Can I at least play while you watch the damn stars?"

"Just don't block my view." Liam wasn't sure what Drake was hinting at, but he agreed just to get the man to stop pouting.

Drake moved quickly to unzip Liam's pants and pushed them down to his thighs. Drake hooked two fingers in the waistband of Liam's underwear and slid the material down.

Liam felt the cool breeze on his bare cock and gasped. Before he could gather his wits, Drake's lips were on Liam's now hard dick sucking it deep into his mouth. "Fuck," Liam whispered, still intent on watching the sky but finding it difficult to concentrate.

"Gonna make you come down my throat first. Then I'll slide deep into your ass and make you see stars one way or another." Drake's words were whispered caresses on Liam's dick.

"Nnngh," Liam moaned. He let Drake taste, tease, suck, and worship his cock. Liam thrust his hips as he wrapped one hand in Drake's dark hair. "Don't want to come yet," he ground out.

"Better hope a star shoots soon or yours will be shooting." Drake tongued Liam's slit before trailing his tongue under Liam's balls.

Three trails of light traveled through the night sky.

Liam gasped. Mostly from the excitement of seeing three shooting stars. Only slightly from the pleasure of Drake's tongue on his balls. *Yeah, right.* "Holy fuck, three of them. I saw three of them." Liam pumped his hips and growled when Drake returned to swallowing his dick. "No more sucking, it's time for fucking."

"Ah, my little star pupil is a poet and didn't know it." Drake rolled to his back and stripped his pants down before pulling his shirt over his head. "Gonna make my own shooting star, make you shoot all over my chest." Drake grabbed a condom from his discarded jeans and rolled it down his length. "Ride me."

Liam felt the command straight to his dick. He pulled his shirt off quickly and pushed his pants the rest of the way off before he straddled Drake's hips. "Lube?" Liam was willing to go the spit route, but lube was always his preference.

Drake rustled through his jeans again and produced a small packet and smeared his cock before teasing a slick finger in and out of Liam's hole.

Liam positioned his ass over Drake's dick and let the wide head slowly invade his body. "So big. Damn." Liam hissed as Drake's cock slipped past his body's tight ring. The sting was always breathtaking and so welcome. As his body adjusted to Drake, Liam began to rock his ass in rhythm to Drake's thrusting hips.

"Fucking hot and tight, so damn tight," Drake growled. "Jack yourself and come on me."

Liam's rhythm faltered when Drake's cock brushed the nerves deep inside his ass, but he gripped his dick and began to stroke as he watched Drake's face lit by the moon's glow. "Harder," Liam begged, his hand never slowing on his cock.

Drake gripped Liam's hips hard enough Liam knew he'd have the marks to show for it in the morning and planted his feet before pistoning his hips to slam his cock deep inside Liam's ass.

Liam threw his head back, still pumping his cock. One, two, three more thrusts and pumps and Liam lost himself, spurting all over Drake's chest. Liam knew the moment Drake came, his cock wedged deep in Liam's ass as it throbbed his release.

Several moments later, once Liam had caught his breath, he groaned. "Did we bring anything to clean up with?"

Drake swatted his ass. "I came prepared." He rolled from the blanket to grab a plastic container of disposable wipes.

They cleaned themselves up and pulled their clothes back on.

"Not sure the night is warm enough for naked outside sleeping." Liam snuggled against Drake's chest and sighed. Had he ever been this relaxed and content? How did one man make him so deliriously happy?

"Naked outside sleeping when the neighbors have curious grandkids may not even be the greatest idea in the heat of summer." Drake chuckled. "The only reason this was okay is because I knew the grandkids weren't visiting. Don't want adventurous kids coming to explore and finding more than they bargained for."

Liam laughed. "Also, as much as I loved the stars and sex, the heat and humidity mixed with grass and bugs doesn't exactly sound like a sexy scene." Liam kissed Drake's jawline.

"Agreed." Drake's arm tightened around Liam's shoulders. "We can always do blanket on the lakeshore to watch stars and then head inside for airconditioned sexy time during the summer. Of course, with the unpredictable Midwest weather, the weather could be anywhere from heat wave, cold snap, or thunderstorms. But we'll make do."

"Sounds amazing."

"You know what sounds even more amazing?" Drake ran his fingers through Liam's hair.

"Hmmm?"

"Knowing you'll be back here with me in the summer."

Liam smiled and pressed his cheek against Drake's warm body. "Nowhere else I'd rather be."

Drake kissed the top of Liam's head.

Liam drifted off to sleep with the thump of Drake's heart and the frogs as his lullaby.

THE WEEKEND HAD BEEN ABSOLUTELY amazing. Not only was the sex mind blowing, the conversation and time spent together was truly life altering; Liam knew his life would never be the same after the time he'd spent with Drake. Liam had felt his absence the moment Drake dropped him off at his apartment. He spent the evening doing laundry and trying not to mope.

Late that night, Liam smiled at the lovey text from Drake. No, they hadn't declared their love for each other; maybe they weren't at that point. But Drake was sweet and Liam definitely felt wanted. When Liam replied with smiley faces with heart eyes, Drake's number immediately appeared on his phone.

"You better still be at work, Detective. You slacked enough this weekend." Liam grinned like a fool as he continued getting ready while talking to Drake.

"Someone kept me busy. Totally worth it." Drake's voice was soft and gravely. "I'm still at work. You home?"

"Yeah. But I'm heading to Shadow Woods here in a bit."

"Why?"

"I need some measurements. Also need to check on the progress and the concrete, see if we're ready for the next phase."

"Want me to meet you there?"

Was it Liam's imagination or did Drake sound hopeful?

"Nah, I just need to grab the numbers and run a few checks. I won't even be there that long. Plus, a dead body at the site is plenty. We don't need to add public indecency to the list."

Drake laughed. "Fine. Text me when you're back home..." His words trailed off.

"Or?"

Drake cleared his throat. "Or you could come spend the night here. If you wanted."

"It's already late. Don't you need to be at work early tomorrow morning? Plus, you're not even home yet." Liam chewed on his lip, biting back a smile and enjoying the warmth that spread through his chest.

"Just a thought. Invitation is open. Anytime." Drake's words rushed out. "I know that sounds desperate or pathetic. I'm not begging you to come to me. Just want you to know I'd love to have you at my place. In my bed. Sleep be damned."

Liam swallowed thickly. "Good to know."

He might as well have floated to his truck. He couldn't wipe the damn giddy smile off his face on the drive to Shadow Woods. *Damn it, you're not a fucking middle schooler in the throes of first love. Knock it off.* But the smile just grew wider.

The first thing Liam did when he arrived at the apartment complex was pull up the hourly and job assignment program on his laptop before he left his truck. Drake's suggestion that Dave looked suspicious had been niggling at the back of his mind for days. Surely there was proof that Dave wasn't worth looking at as a suspect.

Thirty minutes later, Liam's heart thumped. Dave had actually left some top notch *and* top paying jobs to the rest of the crew and opted for only early morning shifts. This had happened multiple times in the recent past, but it also appeared that Dave had done the same switching for the upcoming week. Why would the man give up the higher paying jobs for the early morning shit jobs? Liam's stomach twisted. He may not know Dave very well, but he definitely didn't want to think of him being arrested for murder.

That thought gave Liam pause. He didn't want to see Dave in trouble. Liam didn't even think about the fact that Dave may have been killing people. In his heart, Liam hadn't even given the dead a second thought. They were evil, child predators who didn't deserve to live. If Dave was killing sexual predators, Liam couldn't really hate him for it. But he definitely didn't want Dave arrested for murder. He sighed. Here was proof Dave had switched shifts a lot recently. Should he share the information with Drake? Or stay out of it? While neither option seemed great, Drake already had Dave on his radar because of what the crew had told him. Liam opted to not get involved.

He spent the next twenty minutes gathering measurements before walking the property to check the newest concrete pours. At the last form, the hair on the back of Liam's neck stood on end. There was a rustling behind him at the edge of the woods.

Slipping into the shadows, Liam squinted into the darkness. Probably just an animal.

Liam's heart froze when he saw Eric, the apartment manager, emerging from the woods.

Liam stepped into the light, no plan of what he wanted to say.

Eric startled and froze. "Jesus, you scared the shit out of me. What the hell are you doing out here this late?"

"Could ask you the same." Liam crossed his arms. "I'm

checking the concrete forms and getting some measurements."

The two men stared at each other for several beats.

"You?"

Eric frowned. "Just walking. Couldn't sleep. Trying to keep my mind off some stuff."

"Sorry to hear that. No good when your mind keeps you from sleeping."

"Yeah, lost a family member—a child—not too long ago. My brain and heart just have a hard time shutting down." Eric repositioned his cap and wiped his hands on his pants.

"Hope your walk helped. I'm gonna go. Take it easy." Liam nodded and headed toward his truck. His heart hurt for the guy; losing a family member was never easy, especially a child.

7

DRAKE

DRAKE TOOK a long pull from the beer and laid his head on the back of the couch. He smiled softly when Liam leaned against him.

Drake had been pleased beyond reason when Liam showed up late the night before after he left the construction site. He'd opened the door and pulled Liam into a hug and a deep kiss before leading him to the bedroom where they fell immediately asleep.

And now, Liam was back at Drake's place after they'd both finished at work.

"Tired?" Liam nuzzled at his neck.

"So damn tired. Thought a restful vacation was supposed to help, but it just made me behind at work and had me longing for the lake house." Drake took another sip. "How are your projects going?"

"Still behind schedule, but getting caught up a little each day." Liam rested a hand on Drake's thigh. "How are the cases? I saw on the news that the other two bodies were identified and also sexual predators?" Liam's words were clipped, his jaw tight.

"Yeah, the three men killed were all on the registered sex offender list." Drake ran a hand over his face. "I know your feelings on that, but…"

Liam interrupted, "Honestly, I'm so damn tired right now, I'd rather not even talk about it. We'll have to agree to disagree for now."

Drake sighed, honestly relieved. "You wanting to go out for dinner? 'Cause I gotta tell ya, I could do with some delivery and bed." Drake's head lolled toward Liam. He knew his eyes and smile were tired. Hell, his whole body was tired.

"Delivery and bed sound amazing."

"Great. You want to grab a shower first? I'll call in the order. You know where the towels are. I can probably be done before the food gets here." Drake stood and moved toward the kitchen to sort through take-out menus. "You want pizza? Chinese? Pub?"

"Pub. Fish, cheeseburger, fries." Liam kissed Drake's cheek.

"Sounds good. Hurry up." Drake's heart clenched a little as he watched Liam's sexy ass saunter away. "And don't use up all the hot water!" He laughed when Liam gave him the middle finger.

Once the food order was placed, Drake cleared clothes from his bed and turned down the blankets. He turned the television on and dimmed the lights. The two men had spent more time at Liam's place, but Drake was beginning to enjoy having Liam in his apartment.

"It's all yours," Liam announced as he walked into the

bedroom running a towel through his hair. He was very naked. "How long on the food?"

"Should be here in about twenty." Drake gritted his teeth and adjusted his cock. "No need to get dressed. I plan to keep you naked and in my bed until morning."

"I like the sound of that." Liam made a show of caressing his dick. "Do I need to pay or tip?" He tossed the towel over an armchair.

"I got it." Drake pulled Liam close, his front to Liam's back, and kissed his neck. "But if I'm not out when they get here, put some damn clothes on before you go to the door. I'd prefer all this," he ran his hands up and down Liam's naked torso, "for my eyes only."

Liam laughed. "But you told me to stay naked."

Drake smacked Liam's ass. "I'll be done before they're here."

And he was. Quickest shower he'd ever taken. He walked back toward the bedroom with the food and stripped from his tank and basketball shorts.

"I seriously can't believe I've sunk so low as to eat an entire meal in my bed," Drake grumbled.

"I promise I won't make a mess." Liam climbed into bed. "At least no more of a mess than what we're going to make in a little bit. The sheets will need washed either way."

Drake nodded. "Truth. I'd just rather not find a fry stuck to your ass or an onion ring under my balls."

Liam laughed. "I don't know. Could be fun." He began dividing up the food.

"Can I ask you something?" Drake asked around a mouthful of cheeseburger.

"You just did." Liam popped a fry in his mouth.

"Smart ass."

"Fine, ask away." Liam bit into his fish and sighed. "Best fish sandwich. Ever."

Drake sobered. He knew what he was going to ask Liam could set the night on its ear. "What happened to you when you were little? To land you in foster care, I mean."

Liam froze. Then finished chewing. Then swallowed. And froze again.

"I'm sorry. I shouldn't have asked. You don't have to tell me anything you're not comfortable with." Drake took Liam's hand and squeezed.

"No, it's okay. Just wasn't the question I was expecting."

"What were you expecting?" Drake cocked a brow.

"Honestly, I'm not even sure. It just wasn't that." Liam wiped his mouth with a paper napkin.

"Sorry. I shouldn't have brought it up. I didn't mean to put you on the spot." Drake was curious, but he hated the thought of making Liam retell a painful story.

Liam shook his head. "No, no. It's really okay. I don't tell a lot of people about my past. But you're different; I have no problem telling you."

Drake leaned over and kissed him then rested his forehead against Liam's. "Thank you. It means a lot that you'd trust me with your past."

"It's not pretty, I'll warn you of that right now. It's pretty damn ugly is what it is. You sure you want to hear it?" Liam's eyes were dark as he looked at Drake.

Drake nodded. "I don't want to think of anything hurting you, but I want to know every thing about you."

Liam's next words were a whisper. "Promise it won't make you disgusted by me? Run away from me?"

Drake wrapped a hand around the back of Liam's neck. "Fuck that shit. Never."

Liam drew in a deep breath and sighed. "Okay. Here goes. I loved my mom more than anything, but I figured out really quickly that she had issues a lot of other moms didn't have. My mom always picked boyfriends over me. Drugs, her next fix, always came before me. She wasn't physically *abusive*, but she was neglectful, especially when she was high. And she was always high on something. Meth, coke, ice, whatever she could get her hands on. I'm honestly not sure how I survived being an infant because she wasn't good at taking care of me."

Drake's heart squeezed painfully, knowing the story was likely going to get worse. He held Liam close.

"While my mom never laid a hand on me, the constant traffic of loser boyfriends and drug dealers through our house were a different story. If I wasn't locked in a closet or shoved in a dog crate, I was being slapped around, burned with cigarettes, and threatened with worse if I got in the way. I longed for being ignored and overlooked. It was scary when she disappeared for days at a time, but at least I didn't have to worry about the men."

Drake's jaw ached from gritting his teeth so hard, and his throat felt thick.

"Mom was always desperate for another fix or a rent payment. She just told me to be a good boy when the men were around. She wasn't usually around when the men got physical, but she definitely did nothing to protect me. Seemed like she thought telling me to be good would take care of it."

"How the fuck did she think those men hurting you was okay?" Drake growled out.

Liam shrugged against Drake's body. "I don't know. DCS was called so many times; probably more times than I even knew about. The social workers and caseworkers were overworked and underpaid. Maybe also blind and ignorant because, even if reports got filed, nothing ever happened. Until..." Liam paused, his words thick with pain and hurt.

Drake heard the emotion in Liam's words. He didn't want to hear what Liam said next, but he didn't interrupt.

"Until my mom started dating the scariest motherfucker I'd ever seen. I knew he was bad news the first time Mom brought him home. And I knew there was nothing I could do about it. He was rough and mean with Mom, but he was more interested in me. He didn't hit me, didn't lock me in the closet. But one night, my mom was so strung-out he didn't go to her, he didn't go out, he came to my room. I had locked the door, but he took the doorknob off." Liam shuddered and his nostrils flared. "He was the reason I was finally put into foster care. I tried to clean myself up the best I could, but the emotional and physical pain were both noticed at school the next day. DCS was called as standard protocol for mandatory reporters such as school employees. I was pulled from class to answer questions. The system took me from school and I never saw my mom again."

Drake kissed Liam's head and choked out, "God, baby, I'm so damn sorry that happened." He wanted to hold Liam close forever and try to heal his pain.

"A lot of the foster homes were pretty shitty, but they kept me away from a sexual predator. I got passed from place to place *so* many times. But then I got a miracle. I got a true home. Parents who seemed happy to have me there. They took care of me and spent time with me. Dad taught me all about construction. The system failed me for a long time, and it's failed so many others. But it also saved my life." Liam's last words were whispered.

"Babe, I'm going to hold you for a while. Then, and only if you're in the right headspace for anything physical, I'm going to tease, kiss, and lick you all over. And then I'll take you so soft and slow that you'll be begging for release." Drake kissed the top of Liam's head. "But…"

"But?"

"But first, I need to tell you something. It's going to seem like I'm saying it only because of your story, but I can't *not* say it right now." Drake lifted Liam's chin and looked him in the eyes. "I love you. Not a sympathy or pity type of love. I love having you by my side. I love having you in my arms. I love having you in my bed. I love having you in my life. I love you." Drake kissed Liam's lips softly. "I love you." He kissed Liam again. "I don't know how it happened. I'm not even sure *when* it happened. But it's true."

Drake's heart raced as Liam's eyes blinked back tears.

Liam took a deep, shuddering breath. "I love you, Drake. After the pain of my past, after thinking I was broken and not deserving of real love, I settled for quick and easy hook-ups. But from the very beginning, it's been different with you."

Drake kissed Liam again, his tongue plunging deep. "Don't let me ever hear you say you're broken or don't deserve real love. You are perfect and you deserve every single ounce of real love I plan on giving to you."

Liam snorted. "Was that an innuendo?"

Drake replayed his words before laughing. "No, but I do plan on giving you every single bit of my love." He kissed Liam's ear. "Thrust," he nibbled at Liam's lip, "by thrust," he licked along Liam's jawline, "by thrust." Drake rolled Liam to his back and spread Liam's legs wide before situating himself between Liam's thighs. "You still okay with no condoms since we both got tested?" Drake was *so* damn glad they'd both taken the time to go see their respective doctors recently.

Liam shivered and nodded. "God, yes."

Drake grabbed a bottle of lube from the side table and slicked himself before teasing Liam's hole and sliding in first one finger and then another.

"Please," Liam begged.

Drake obliged by pressing his rock hard cock against Liam's entrance and pushing in slowly. He moaned in pleasure as Liam's body opened for him. "So fucking tight, so hot." He slid the rest of the way inside as Liam wrapped his legs around Drake's waist. Drake leaned in close and kissed Liam's parted lips. "You're so good, so perfect, and I love you so much."

Liam whimpered into the kiss. "I love you. So damn much."

Drake thrust in slow, powerful strokes while ravaging Liam's mouth with his own. He nudged the ball of nerves deep in Liam's body and knew his boyfriend was close. Which was good as his own orgasm was building. Drake lifted Liam's left leg and pressed it toward Liam's chest while he continued to pump deep into Liam's body.

Liam's hands palmed Drake's face and their eyes met.

Drake took each of Liam's hands one at a time and

placed them above Liam's head. Liam strained to move his arms, but Drake held firm. His thrusts increased in power and speed, and Liam half grunted, half whimpered under him.

Drake gripped Liam's hands. "I want you to come. I want to feel it, want to hear it, want to spill my cum inside of you."

Liam threw his head back, his whole body tensing as he moaned his release.

Drake's breath caught when Liam's hot seed splattered between them. With a final, hard thrust deep into Liam's ass, Drake lost control and exploded in long, hot spurts and growled Liam's name as he emptied himself.

Drake's heart throbbed in his ears, his chest heaved as he tried to catch his breath, and his hot skin shivered as cool air met with sweat. "Oh my God. That was beyond amazing. You're so damn good." Drake kissed Liam. "I love you. And I'm not just saying that because the sex is spectacular."

Liam laughed. "I love you, too. And I *am* saying that because you just destroyed me. But also because I just plain ol' love you."

"Awww, such a sweet talker." Drake pulled slowly from Liam's body and rolled from the bed. "Wipe down or shower?"

"Wipe down, sleep, shower later," Liam mumbled, his eyes closed.

"Good plan." Drake walked to the bathroom and tossed a washcloth to Liam. "But don't think I'm done with you."

"Oh yeah? Have a plan do you?" Liam cracked an eye.

Drake realized his face must have had his feelings written all over it because Liam propped up on an elbow.

"What's up?" Liam frowned.

Drake ran a hand over his face. "Would you ever consider topping?"

Liam's eyes went wide. "Topping? You?"

Drake knew his face was flushed, but he simply nodded. "Yeah. It's not a deal breaker; I love what we're doing. But I want that with you. If you're willing."

Liam nodded. "Definitely. I'm not an exclusive bottom."

"Then I think we know what's next on our agenda." Drake winked.

"I think we're both going to be useless at work tomorrow."

"Definitely." Drake wrapped Liam in his arms and they fell asleep.

Drake came into consciousness a couple hours later to a delicious warmth surrounding his body and rolling hips against his ass. "You have something on your mind?" His gravely words filled the moonlit room.

"You. Spread open for me. Taking my cock deep." Liam's arm went around Drake's chest and pulled him close as he whispered in Drake's ear. "You're the one who put the bug in my ear and now I can't stop thinking about it." Liam's hand caressed Drake's naked chest and tweaked a nipple.

Drake groaned.

"You like that?" Liam purred and toyed with Drake's nipples.

"Yesss," Drake hissed.

Liam rolled Drake to his back and straddled his chest. "I want you to swallow my cock first."

Drake grunted and opened wide for Liam's hard length to slide between his lips. His lips felt stretched, his throat threatened to gag, and his eyes stung with tears. But Drake let Liam fuck his face for several minutes until Liam gasped and pulled away.

"Too close. I want to be in your ass when I come." Liam leaned over the side of the bed and grabbed the earlier discarded bottle of lube. "You know, when I was younger, I was of the mind that spit was a quality lube."

Drake smirked. "And now?"

Liam smiled in the moonlight. "It will do in a pinch. But if actual lube is available, I'm not going to turn it down."

"Same," Drake agreed. "Especially in this instance." He gritted his teeth as Liam teased a slick finger into Drake's tight hole. "Oh Jesus. It's been a good while since I've done this."

"No worries. I'll go slow. It may burn, but it'll be a good burn," Liam teased as he added a second finger.

Drake writhed on the bed as he reveled in the sting of Liam's invasion. After several moments, Drake gasped out, "I need you. Now. Do it now."

"Bossy. I knew you'd be trying to top from the bottom. Patience." Liam continued to play with Drake's hole, stretching him a slight bit more with each passing minute. Then Liam leaned forward and kissed Drake. "You ready for me?"

Drake nodded and kissed Liam deeply. When the plump head of Liam's slick cock nudged Drake's entrance, he tensed but only for a moment. This was Liam. Liam loved him and he loved Liam. Drake had asked for this; he wanted this. He took a deep breath and pressed against Liam's slow invasion. The initial sting became a slow burn which faded into only a slight discomfort. "Fuck. You're big," Drake gritted out.

"And you're so damn tight I may blow right here and now." Liam paused mid-thrust and took a deep breath.

"Do it, fuck me. Make it hard." Drake put his hands behind his knees and spread himself open even more.

Liam's groan turned into a whimper as he found a rhythm sliding hard and deep into Drake's body.

Drake loved the feeling of Liam's balls smacking against his ass, the rub of Liam's abdomen against Drake's throbbing cock, and Liam's hot breath against his ear whispering, "So damn tight. So good. Fuck. God damn it, Drake, I'm gonna come."

"Do it," Drake demanded as he reached to stroke his own erection. "Fill me. I want to feel you in me all day tomorrow."

Liam arched his back and moaned as he emptied himself into Drake.

Drake cried out as he erupted between them just as Liam filled him with spurts of liquid heat.

"Oh, fucking hell," Liam groaned. "I'm not going to be able to walk tomorrow."

"You? I'm not sure my legs will ever return to their normal position." Drake laughed and kissed Liam. "Have I told you how much I love you?"

"Tell me again." Liam batted his lashes.

"I love you." Drake kissed him. "Have I told you how fucking crazy and not planned it is for me to be in love with you?"

"I kinda figured that out." Liam smiled.

"But I can't stop it. You rolled over me like one of those damn steamrollers and I had no chance. Hook, line, and sinker. I'm done." Drake winced when Liam pulled from his body.

"Such a sweet talker," Liam teased. "Shower?"

"Yeah. Then we'd better actually sleep since we do have jobs to report to tomorrow."

After showers, Drake pulled Liam into his arms and kissed him. "Sleep tight. I love you."

Liam murmured, "Mmmm, love you too."

8

LIAM

LIAM STRETCHED his neck and back as he climbed from the truck at the Shadow Woods site. If he and Drake were going to be having sleepovers on work nights, they'd need to figure out a better sleep routine. He smiled to himself. Not that he was complaining about the previous night's activities, but damn, he was exhausted. Between being tired and the cold, wet bite in the air, he was grateful for the very large cup of coffee he'd stopped to buy on the way to work.

He pulled out his digital tablet, the rolls of blueprints, and his laptop and went to work setting up his *office* in the bed of his truck. He often appreciated the ease of the digital blueprints, but sometimes there was no denying that a physical print was still better. Glancing around the site as trucks pulled in and workers began to gather, Liam noticed that Dave Houston and his concrete truck were nowhere to be seen.

What the hell?

Liam pulled up the schedule and saw that, once again,

Dave had opted out of a couple bigger, better paying jobs and taken several smaller, earlier drops. Liam wanted to give the man the benefit of the doubt, but he was definitely making it hard with all the unexplained swaps.

As Liam thought about Dave, his eyes traveled to the latest concrete forms. His gaze came to an abrupt stop when he saw Eric standing by the concrete.

What the actual hell was going on? He hadn't had enough sleep, Dave was mysteriously taking crappy jobs and was already late, and now Eric Cooper was hanging around the concrete? Liam ran a hand over his face as he breathed out several curse words. With a fortifying sip of his coffee, Liam headed toward the concrete forms.

Eric seemed deep in thought and hadn't heard Liam's approach. "Hey, man," Liam called out.

The property manager jumped about a foot before turning toward Liam with wide eyes. "Oh, hey," Eric rushed out as he shoved his hands in his pockets. "Sorry, couldn't sleep. Took a walk and ended up here."

"You doing okay?" Liam noticed Eric's bloodshot eyes and haggard appearance.

"Honestly? No," Eric mumbled.

Liam nodded, giving Eric time to talk if he wanted.

"I saw on the news that the police said all the bodies were sexual predators. Did you see that?" Eric stared at the concrete wall.

"I did," Liam answered.

"Seems like maybe it's not such a bad thing, ya know?"

Liam's pulse quickened. "Yeah?"

Eric was quiet for several moments. "Had a family member, a little kid, who was sexually abused. All predators are scum and deserve to suffer. That's my take."

"Can't say I disagree," Liam offered.

"Just thinking a lot about it. Not sure the police need to worry about the deaths if they're all shitbags who hurt innocent kids." Eric shrugged and hunched deeper into his jacket. "I've got a list of repairs I need to get to. Can't sleep at night because of the nightmares, can't sleep during the day because people are counting on me. Guess I'll sleep when I'm dead." He gave a slight nod and wave and walked through the damp dirt toward the front of the complex.

Liam watch the man leave. Was he acting weird? Or just a person in the throes of mourning? Liam's attention was diverted by the grumble of an engine as a concrete truck pulled in.

About damn time.

Liam's gaze followed the truck as Dave drove it straight to the needed spot, hollered a few directions at the men on the ground, and began the pour. Based on the schedule, Dave was only about twenty minutes late, but it bothered Liam. He expected his crew on time and if they couldn't be on time, he expected them to talk to him about it. Not just change their schedules without a word. To be fair, Liam allowed the permanent crew to change their schedules as needed as long as they assured there was always a full crew to work the job. But most of them ran it past him first. Dave dropping bigger, better jobs for the crappy, early morning ones was eating at Liam for some reason.

As Dave drove by several moments later, Liam waved him down.

Dave stopped the truck and lowered his window. "Morning," he offered.

"Got a minute?" Liam asked.

Dave hesitated. "Got another job to get to, don't want to be late."

Liam raised a brow.

"Sorry about this morning, got caught up and started late."

"Will only take a minute," Liam stated, giving Dave no option but to climb down from the truck. "You doing okay?"

Dave was slightly older than Liam, but looked like he'd aged two decades since the last time he and Liam had been face-to-face. "Sure, just busy. Not sleeping great. Kids wear us out; baby keeps us hoppin' that's for sure."

Liam nodded. "Noticed you've been dropping a lot of jobs for the earlier ones. Not that I mind, but you're losing out on some of the bigger pay and the early gigs can't be great for your sleep."

"It's working fine," Dave snapped. "Sorry, no disrespect. Just got a lot going on. Need the early drops if possible. Hope that's not a problem?"

Liam studied Dave's tired eyes, his jittery movements, the agitation. "Nothing illegal going on, right? Can't have that on my crew." Was Dave killing people? Helping to bury the bodies? Doing drugs? Hell, Liam wasn't sure and hated that he was beginning to suspect everyone he came in contact with.

Dave frowned. "Illegal? No, man. It's all good. I've got it handled."

"We've got a lot of eyes scrutinizing our every move right now. Just don't want you calling unwarranted attention to yourself or the company."

Dave stared hard at Liam before glancing at his watch

and toward the truck. "I really need to get going so I can get this last pour done." When Liam nodded, Dave all but ran to the truck.

Something was definitely up with him, but what?

Liam spent the rest of the day up to his ears in work. Nothing went wrong, just a lot of shit they had to do along with working around the investigation. For the most part, they were allowed to move on as needed, but the constant checks to be sure they could take their next steps were getting really old really fast.

By the time Liam walked into his apartment that evening, he was ready to crash. His mind was all over the place with Eric and Dave, but he didn't want to bring it up with Drake.

Why?

He didn't want an argument.

He didn't want to stress Drake even more.

He didn't want to cast suspicion on the two men. If they were doing something wrong, the police would figure it out. Right?

Be honest with yourself. Liam sighed. Maybe the biggest reason he didn't go to Drake was that he really couldn't see how it was a problem if sexual predators were being killed.

Killing was wrong. Liam understood that. But so was abusing, molesting, and raping. If the monsters doing that were finally getting punished? Liam really didn't see how that was so wrong.

His phone buzzed.

Drake: *You coming over? I'll pick up some food on the way home.*

Home. Liam stared at the word. How could being with

Drake feel so right, the word *home* be so accurate, yet they had such a huge divide between them when it came to these murders?

Was it just something they'd need to agree to disagree on? Keep work and personal life separate? Liam and Drake were a great match in almost every way except that one point of contention. Liam pushed aside the thoughts of Eric and Dave, took a deep breath to clear his head of his and Drake's conflict, and tapped out a text.

Liam: *Yeah, just came home to shower and grab a few things. I'll be over in a bit.*

As Liam showered, he thought about all the time he was spending at Drake's. He loved being there, but he sometimes felt that he was throwing away rent on his place if he was never there. Drake wasn't the type to commit and settle down, so the thought of living with him full-time was ludicrous. Right? Would Liam even want that?

Living with Drake? Setting up a life? Falling to sleep and waking in Drake's arms day in and day out? Liam sighed as the water rained down on him. Yeah, that definitely sounded like a life he wanted. Would he prefer a commitment? Sure. But they'd already agreed to be exclusive. Did he need a ring? Liam scoffed at his thoughts and shut off the water a bit harder than necessary. He wanted to live with Drake, yes. But would Drake ever make that step?

Liam shook his head as he dried off. Highly unlikely. *You never thought Drake would see you as anything but a convenient hookup either. Don't write it off just yet. He may surprise you.*

With a roll of his eyes, Liam hung his towel to dry,

brushed his teeth, and stuffed some clothes into an overnight bag. He'd already put a toothbrush in Drake's bathroom. Maybe he could start leaving some clothes there a little at a time.

After checking through his mail for anything important, he stuck a few bills in his bag, made sure he had his laptop, turned on the kitchen light for security reasons—maybe he should get one of those light timers—and locked the door behind him before heading to his truck.

Pizza and beer awaited Liam when he arrived at Drake's place. They ate, chatted about mundane things—both seemed to be avoiding the topic of dead bodies buried in concrete, maybe both were keen to avoid arguments—and Liam slipped into bed while Drake went to shower.

With heavy eyes and scattered thoughts, Liam struggled to stay awake until Drake joined him.

"You've been quiet, you okay?" Drake asked as he tossed his towel onto the bed post, climbed into bed, and pulled Liam close.

"Yeah, just exhausted." Liam rocked his naked ass back and hummed when he connected with Drake's warm, damp skin. "Don't think I can handle strenuous," he began.

"How 'bout just slow and easy, we both get off, and maybe it clears our heads enough to sleep peacefully?" Drake whispered against Liam's ear. "I swear, my head's been so full and stretched lately, I barely know which way is up. Not sure work has ever gotten to me this much."

Liam rocked back again. "It's getting to me, too, and I'm not even the one working the cases. I'm sorry you're so stressed." He shifted slightly, sighing when Drake's now-hard cock nestled between Liam's legs, nudging gently against his balls. "Slow and easy sounds perfect. Touch me?"

Drake murmured softly as he placed kisses along Liam's skin and reached around to take Liam's length in his fist. "Just want to kiss you and feel you come in my hand," he whispered as he slowly thrust his cock between Liam's legs. "Love my dick sliding against your balls," Drake growled and continued the slow rhythm.

Liam's body was trapped in a tortuous slow-burn as Drake's cock skimmed his taint and balls while his fist stroked Liam's shaft. This wasn't hard and heavy, sweaty and breathless, this was slow, soft, and sensual. Liam reached behind to grip Drake's ass and shifted to expose more of his neck to Drake's hot kisses. Liam pumped his hips, enjoying the sensation of Drake's hand on his cock and Drake's dick grazing his balls with each thrust. Time seemed to slow as his release climbed slowly closer to the surface.

Liam turned his head and gasped into Drake's mouth when the man's lips caught and devoured Liam's. The slow plunge of Drake's tongue brought Liam's body to a soft breaking point and he whimpered against Drake's lips as he erupted into Drake's fist.

Drake's thrusting stilled and Liam reveled in the hot stickiness that coated his balls as Drake continued to slide his now-slick cock between Liam's legs.

"That was possibly the softest, sweetest orgasm I've ever had," Liam mused. "We must be *really* tired."

"I'm not going to want that every time, but I love that we can have sex without it having to be porn-worthy all the time." Drake grabbed the towel to clean himself and Liam.

"Porn-worthy?" Liam chuckled. "I'd say we've had a few times that maybe wouldn't make it to the cutting-room floor." His words were already thick with sleep.

"When we're rested, we can try for a top-rated scene," Drake teased. "Love you, but I gotta sleep."

Liam wasn't even sure he responded before he was sound asleep.

By the time morning rolled around, only the barest peek of sun beginning to show through the blinds, Liam woke with a start. Had he been dreaming? Remembering something? The first night Liam ran into Eric walking out of the woods, had that been a shovel in the man's hands or just a walking stick? The day before, when Liam had seen Eric at the concrete wall, did the property manager hide something in his pocket? Or was Liam imagining things? He ran a hand over his sleep-lined face. Eric had as much reason to want sexual predators dead as Liam, but Liam—while not upset the monsters were dead—wasn't killing people. Would Eric? He had access to the site. He had reason.

Liam's head swirled. Then again, Dave Houston also had access and had been acting differently. Would a father and husband risk it all to kill? And what would his reasoning be? Did Dave have the same past as Liam? A painful story like Eric?

"I can almost hear your brain grinding gears over there," Drake grumbled. "What's up?"

Liam tensed. "Just thinking about jobs that need to be done today. Already behind and, even if we get every job done today—which is highly unlikely—we'll still be behind. Every day we're behind is loss of money for me, for my men, for the company. Plus, it makes us look bad. Just a lot to think about."

"I'm sorry. I know you're in a frustrating position." Drake pulled Liam close and kissed his cheek. "Let's shower and grab breakfast before both of our crazy days have to get started."

Liam smiled and relaxed into Drake's embrace. Even if they were stretched thin at work and butting heads about the right or wrong of the bodies, Liam appreciated having Drake by his side. But damn, he was ready for these cases to be solved and things to go back to *normal*. Whatever his and Drake's normal may be.

An hour or so later, after a very enjoyable shower *and* breakfast with Drake, Liam sipped his coffee as he parked at the front of Shadow Woods and climbed from his truck with a second coffee in hand. Without knowing exactly which apartment was Eric's, Liam walked into the office in hopes that the property manager would be there.

"Good morning, what can I do..." Eric stopped short when he came from the back room and saw Liam standing at the desk. "What?"

"Don't mean to interrupt your work," Liam began. "Just wanted to ask you for a favor."

Eric narrowed his eyes. "What?"

Liam chuckled. The guy clearly wasn't thrilled to see him. "Brought you a coffee." He held the cup out toward Eric.

Eric took the coffee and took a cautious sip. "Thanks. Is that all?"

Liam ran a hand through his hair. "Actually, wanted to talk a bit about yesterday." When Eric continued to sip his coffee and didn't object, Liam continued. "Look, I get where you're coming from. I have a really ugly past and I agree that those monsters need to be punished." Liam took a drink and eyed Eric over his cup. "But I need you to stay away from the concrete. For work to be done and to keep yourself out of trouble, just stay away from the site, okay?"

Eric's cheeks reddened and he cocked his chin. "What am I, some sort of nuisance just because I like to take walks to clear my head? Keep myself out of trouble? What exactly are you implying?"

"Look, I want them to hurt as much as you do, but you gotta…" Liam trailed off.

Eric slammed the coffee cup down on the desk. "I've got enough stress and grief going on right now, I don't need more from the damned construction foreman. We're done here."

Liam frowned. "I just…"

"Done. See yourself out." Eric gestured toward the door before disappearing behind a side door.

"Well, that went well," Liam muttered to himself as he climbed back into his truck and drove toward the back of the complex.

Liam spent the rest of the day throwing himself into his work. The only thing that kept him smiling was looking forward to the date he and Drake had planned. Nothing big or fancy, but they were going to get home from work at a normal time, shower, and go out for dinner rather than crashing with take-out on the couch. It wasn't a huge deal, but Liam was excited about it.

"DAMN IT," Drake growled as he slammed down the receiver on his desk phone. In the process of throwing a hissy fit, he knocked over his coffee cup. "Fuuuuck!" Drake stalked across the hall to the tiny breakroom and grabbed a roll of paper towel and a bottle of cleaning spray.

Muttering obscenities the whole time, Drake cleaned up the mess he'd made before stomping back across the hall to toss the cleaning supplies back where they belonged.

He threw himself into his chair and let loose a frustrated growl and fisted a chunk of hair. The pain was enough of a distraction that Drake was able to take a few deep breaths and *almost* push away the most recent thing that pissed him off. The spilled coffee was easier to get over than the rest of the shit that he was dealing with.

Drake ran a hand over his face and groaned. He was so damn exhausted and so pissed off. Clues and tips and evidence were collected, still being collected, and pouring in on the tip line, but Drake wasn't getting the matches he was looking for. He needed something bigger, the big piece of the puzzle that seemed to be missing. Drake was a damned good detective and he was accustomed to most cases panning out exactly the way he needed them to.

Except that last one. The one that went to Mathers in Cold Case. The one Mathers still gave him shit about.

Fuck. Maybe Drake was losing his touch. Was he done? Washed-up? Mathers indicated it daily. Was he right? Fuck that, Mathers and his team hadn't solved the cold case either. The man was simply an irritating prick in general, no need for Drake to put any stock in Mathers' words.

He breathed deeply. All he really wanted was to get a break in these damn bodies-in-concrete cases, wrap them all up, and dig out from underneath the paperwork. Drake turned in his chair to study his notes—page after page after page of notes. The three bodies had a few things in common. Drinking, some petty crimes, lived in or around the Indy area most of their lives, but the main thing that stuck out were all three dead men had been sex offenders. Multiple sexual offenses. Against children.

Drake wanted something, *anything* but that to tie them together. All his life, Drake had known right and wrong. He was a champion for right and a punisher of wrong. Killing was wrong. Period. And he would work these damned cases until they were solved and the killer was punished. But Liam's story, the pained expression on his face and the hurt in his words, haunted Drake each and every day that he found nothing to connect the bodies except for their heinous crimes against children. Drake would work to see the killer brought in, but it got harder and harder each day to clearly see the wrong in monsters meeting their end. Drake had never lived in the gray area between right and wrong. Until Liam. And now, the lines were blurred and Drake's head and heart were at odds over where right ended and wrong began in these cases.

He huffed. "Fuck, stop it," Drake chastised himself. "Someone is *killing* other humans. No matter what those men did, it's not right for a person to murder. Period." *But those men hurt children. Men like that hurt Liam. What punishments did they get for destroying children? A bit of time in jail with meals and a place to sleep? A slap on the wrist? Then let loose to prey on their victims again and again?*

Drake slammed his fist on the desk. "Stop letting your heart get involved. Two wrongs don't make a right." He hated what had happened to Liam, hated what happened to all victims of sexual abuse. But hating those things and wanting them to stop didn't mean that murder was suddenly acceptable. Drake could look past a lot of things. Maybe his moral compass wasn't *as* strong as he'd once thought because he had no issues with wanting every offender to hurt and suffer in the same way as their victims—hell, multiply it by ten. But murder was still murder and he'd taken an oath to serve and protect. He was bound to catch the bad guys and bring them to their due consequences.

Yeah, but those dead men deserved consequences as well. When the system didn't work, maybe your killer did the world a favor.

Drake's head swam with thoughts of right and wrong, black and white, gray areas, pain and suffering, justice, responsibility, and Liam. *Liam.* Damn it. Drake hated that Liam was somewhat caught in the middle of this mess. Hated that they had such differing views—but really, were Drake's views subject to change the more he fell in love with Liam? Could he still be a good detective if loving someone made him question his morals? Made the line between right and wrong so blurry?

He needed reports to come in quicker. He needed evidence to link up and show him *something*. And he definitely needed to solve these cases and bring in the killer before another damn body buried in concrete showed up. He was tired of Mathers indicating the cases would end up cold. Tired of all the media speculation. Tired of reports not holding the information he needed. Just *tired*.

What he really wanted was to walk away and forget everything. Take Liam to the lake house and ignore real life. *And when had he ever wanted to walk away from his job?* Fuck, maybe he really was losing it.

Instead, Drake made a list of reports he needed to check and recheck, calls he needed to make, and vowed to reread every word of his notes even if it took until midnight.

Later, Drake wasn't sure how much time had passed, Simms knocked on the door frame. Drake blinked rapidly as he pulled himself from his work and tried to reorient himself.

"Lewis, you need to go home. Have you eaten or had anything to drink today?" Simms crossed his arms over his chest.

"Had coffee," Drake mumbled.

"This morning? It's five-thirty in the fuckin' evening. Go home."

Drake's eyes grew wide. How the hell had so many hours passed? "Fuck, sorry. Got pulled in on these dead bodies, lost track of time." He ran a hand over his face. "I'll finish up here and then head home."

Simms narrowed his eyes. "You need a life outside of this damn place. Someone to make you want to go home instead of killing yourself here." He gave a small wave and walked away.

Drake's heart plummeted. *Liam*. "Fuck!" He grabbed his personal phone from under a mound of papers. Twenty missed texts and three missed calls. "Fuck, fuck, *fuck!*" He didn't even take time to read the texts or check his voicemail.

Liam picked up on the third ring. "Let me guess."

Okay, he was pissed. Rightfully so.

"I'm so sorry. I got caught up in the case and Simms just pulled me out. I've been buried in paperwork, notes, reports, evidence, tips, since this morning and didn't even realize so much time has passed. I'll make it up to you. We'll reschedule our date."

"Or you could leave now and we can head out, it's not too late," Liam suggested.

Drake took a deep breath and closed his eyes. "As much as I'd love to, I need to stay and finish up this work. If not, I'll start tomorrow even more buried than I am now. I gotta keep working—surely I'll catch a break soon."

"Yeah, okay. Talk to you later," Liam bit out and disconnected.

Drake stared at the screen of his phone and fought the urge to throw it against the wall. He'd told Liam what to expect from him, none of this should have been a surprise. *Doesn't mean it makes the hurt and disappointment any easier.* "Fuck!" Drake launched a pen against the wall. It wasn't as satisfying as a phone or coffee mug, but it was all he was willing to break at that point.

With a pounding head and aching heart, Drake returned to his work, determined to get caught up and find some new answers.

When he pulled into his place several hours later, he was shocked to see Liam's truck there and a light on in the window.

"Hey," Drake said softly when he walked through the door. He glanced at Liam's bag. "You leaving?"

Liam hefted the bag over his shoulder. "Figured I'd get my dirty clothes and shit like that. Get things washed since I don't know when I'll be back here." Liam's words held a challenge.

Drake crossed the room and pulled Liam into his arms. "I'm really sorry about missing our date. I was looking forward to it."

Liam scoffed, but relaxed in Drake's arms.

"I *was*," Drake insisted. "I told you how it gets sometimes with cases and these bodies are giving me fits. I'm beyond stressed, way past exhausted, and feel like I'm racing the clock to make an arrest before another body shows up."

"I guess I just wish you weren't willing to make time for your job, but not for me—and I hate sounding like a whiny, clingy brat, I just miss you and wanted to spend time with you." Liam took a step back.

"You knew what you were getting into," Drake bit out, knowing he wasn't being fair to Liam, but too tired to filter himself.

Liam shook his head. "I just don't understand why

you're working yourself to death for *this*. What's the point? Will it matter in the end?"

"*This* is my job. I'm damned good at what I do and I don't give up on cases. I have a reputation to live up to. Ever since I was promoted to this position, I've had to prove myself over and over because of my age. I'm not going to stop being the best just because I have a boyfriend. I can't and I won't." Drake crossed his arms over his chest.

"So, you mean to tell me you're working your ass off to catch a guy who is ridding the world of the worst of the worst scum?" Liam's words weren't quite loud but were definitely edging that direction.

"He's *killing*. He's breaking the law. He's as bad as his victims." Drake swung his arm in a wild gesture.

"What if the killer was going after the guys who knocked me around as a child?"

"Farfetched." Drake shook his head.

"But *what if*? What if he was to kill that son-of-a-bitch who hurt me so bad?" Liam's words were loaded emotion.

"He's a *killer*." Drake gritted his teeth.

"So, you'd rather catch him, save your job and reputation, maybe get a medal than let a friend, a *boyfriend* —someone you supposedly love—find long awaited vindication all in the name of following the law?"

"Why would my *boyfriend* be so against me solving this case? Maybe you have more vested in it than I thought." Drake's stomach churned even as he said the words. "Access, motive, and sleeping with the detective assigned to the case? Maybe I've been fucking blind *and* stupid this whole time." His nostrils flared and his jaw ached. Drake's heart and head were at war.

You love him, you dumbass. Apologize. Make this right.

Has he kept you from seeing the truth? Are you missing something because of your involvement with Liam? Is he purposely keeping you off the track? Trying to convince you to let the case go because he's involved somehow?

Before Drake could make a decision—hell, he didn't even know what decision he was trying to make—Liam's face flashed hurt and anger.

"Gotcha. I see where I rank. If you decide what we have is more important than your damn job, let me know. Until then, I guess you can spend your time trying to decide if the person you love—who loves you more than anything in this world—is murdering sex offenders." Liam shook his head and shouldered past Drake, slamming the door behind him.

Drake's head was about to explode, his heart truly hurt —a physical pain zinged through his chest—his stomach rolled as if he was going to puke, and his eyes stung with tears. "Fuck," he whispered to himself. "What in the actual fuck did you just do?"

As if on autopilot, Drake undressed, showered, and fell into bed. Had he just lost Liam? For what? His damn job?

No, you have a job to do just like he does. Your job consists of making sure wrongs are punished. This has nothing to do with how you feel about Liam. You need to catch a killer.

Drake took a shuddery breath.

You kinda made it about Liam when you basically accused him of being a killer.

"Fuck!" Drake growled. He needed a break in the case. He needed to be done so he could work things out with Liam. But what about future cases? Would he and Liam be at each other's throats every time they had differing viewpoints on criminals?

Sure that his head or heart would explode before sunrise, Drake closed his eyes and hoped for either an easy ending to his pain or a major break in the case. He needed one of those things to happen or he wasn't sure how he'd keep functioning.

10

LIAM

AFTER A NIGHT of waffling between hurt and pissed—and *zero* sleep—Liam gathered his coffee and work gear and stomped down the stairs to his truck. The night before—the fight with Drake—hung over his head, clung to his heart, suffocated him. On one hand, Liam admired Drake for always being able to see black and white so clearly—he didn't straddle the fence, didn't give in and sacrifice his integrity. On the other hand, Liam was angry that Drake didn't see the difference between an innocent murder victim and a murdered sexual offender. Drake's dismissal of Liam's question regarding what would happen if one of the victims—or potential victims—was one of Liam's past abusers...that shit hurt. Liam kept recalling the way Drake waved off the question as *farfetched.*

Liam wanted Drake to imagine a scenario where he was forced to choose between Liam and doing the "right" thing by shutting down the murder of sex offenders. What would Drake choose? Liam's heart hurt to think Drake wouldn't choose him over the requirements of his job.

Fuck. Was Liam being completely unfair to Drake in asking him to choose? What if the situation was reversed? What if Drake came to Liam and told him he'd been hurt in the past by a steel beam and he needed Liam to stop using steel beams in his construction. Would Liam give up the safety of his buildings, ruin his reputation as a damn good foreman, possibly lose his job to save Drake from his bad past with steel beams?

He ran a hand over his face. It was a shitty analogy. Liam's past was real and painful. Drake's imagined steel beam pain wasn't real. But the hypothetical situation got Liam thinking just outside of his head enough to admit maybe he could understand where Drake was coming from.

That didn't excuse the fight or Drake's dismissal of Liam. It didn't excuse Drake canceling their date. *But it was okay for you to be an hour late getting to Drake's house last week when you had to stay on site later than you'd planned?* Liam growled under his breath and slammed a hand on the steering wheel. That was different. *Was it?* Liam pushed his thoughts aside the best he could as he wheeled into the apartment complex and parked at the front office building.

He climbed from his truck and stalked into Eric's office. Again. Liam had no idea why he was so concerned with Eric. Did he want the man to be the murder suspect? Want him to keep killing? Want him to stop? Want him to be innocent? Liam truly had no clue, but something kept him interested just enough to not let it go.

"Eric?" Liam called out as he followed muddy footprints toward the back room. "You in here?"

The man appeared—drying his hands on a towel—looking seriously irritated to see the foreman. "Why do you keep coming here? I'm trying to do a job."

Liam held up his hands. "Sorry. I don't mean to be a bother. I'm just going through some shit with my own past—seems like I never get away from it—and your comment about having a child in your family who was hurt won't leave my mind."

Eric eyed him suspiciously. "What do you want?"

Liam scowled. "Fuck if I know. I've not been sleeping,"

Eric's snort interrupted. "I know that feeling for sure."

"And I can't get your family member out of my head. I just thought if you ever wanted to talk about it, I can listen. I understand nightmares and how the past can haunt a person."

Eric stared at Liam for so long, Liam started to turn around and leave. After all, he really had no idea why he was even talking to Eric. What good was it going to bring? If Eric wasn't the killer, Liam was just asking him to relive a painful story. If Eric *was* the killer, what was Liam going to do? Turn him in? Encourage him? Ignore it? Maybe Drake had it right by not getting emotionally involved. Black and white, cut and dry, right and wrong, don't let your heart step into the scene. Facts, laws, procedures, stick to those and stay safe, keep others safe.

Eric cleared his throat and Liam turned back around.

He studied Eric for a moment. Could the guy really be a killer? Didn't a person have to be somewhat unhinged to kill—kill *multiple* people? Eric seemed distraught and distracted by his family trauma, but enough to *kill*? Liam raised a brow.

"This past year or so has been really rough. I don't really talk to anyone about it, but it's been eating me up inside. I've been taking steps to work through it, but the pain never leaves." Eric stared out the window. "I was named emergency guardian for my nephew when my sister overdosed. His name was Craig. Great kid. I had high hopes I could adopt him, keep him in our family and let him see his mom as her mental and physical health allowed." He swallowed and clenched his jaw. "The courts always want to reunite a family if possible. I get that, I truly do. But my sister is a drug addict; she had no business having custody of an innocent kid."

Liam's gut rolled as dark memories of his past barreled through him. "Damn man, I'm sorry. I get that, probably more than you could ever know." As a kid, Liam had never wanted to be separated from his mom, he just wanted her to stop allowing all the assholes to walk all over her, use her, and hurt her kid. As an adult, Liam had accepted that his mom wasn't fit to care for herself let alone a young child.

"My sister got pissed at me right around the time I was hoping to be granted permanent custody. She was angry because I wouldn't give her money. Instead of telling the courts she wanted Craig to live with me so she could stay in his life while she got clean and put her life back on track, she begged and pleaded with the judge, gave a big sob story about how a mom needs her child, blah, blah, blah." Eric's fist tapped the counter. "I was prepared to let her be in Craig's life, as his mother, while I made sure he was safe and healthy. And Crissy had agreed to that, she was good with it, happy I could provide for Craig and she could still see him and love him and be part of his life. And then a drug craving hit and she needed money and all went to shit." His voice cracked and he paused. "The judge was visibly hesitant, but sided with Crissy. Craig was returned to her full-time with a warning of 'we're watching and he will be taken away permanently if you so much as allow him a papercut.'" Eric scoffed. "Fuck bunch of good that did. Crissy hooked up pretty quickly with a guy I assumed was able to keep her in drugs. I never got to see or talk to him, but Craig reported he was 'old and disgusting.' Crissy she swore she was in love. Not too long after this guy came into the picture—oh, and Craig was only allowed to call him *Sir*, never heard his real name—my nephew called crying one night, saying Sir hurt him. Before he could tell me what happened, the phone call was cut off. I went over there, but no one was home." He sniffed. "Week later, Craig was dead. Crissy was gone and Craig's body was found in a creek a couple counties over."

Liam knew immediately that the story was going to get even worse.

A tear escaped and ran down Eric's cheek. "Blunt force trauma was the cause of death, but the death report outlined several burns and breaks." He took a deep breath. "And he'd been sexually assaulted."

Bile rose in Liam's throat. "I'm so sorry." Dear God, Craig's story was almost a mirror to Liam's. Craig was let down by the system, by his mother, and violated in the worst of ways by a monster who deserved every bit of punishment available and more. Liam's heart hurt for the lost child and he couldn't help but wonder why he was allowed to be saved from his mom and abusers while Craig was discarded as not worthy. "I'm so, so sorry." It was all Liam could find the words to say.

"I got a letter from Crissy not long after. She rambled on and on about *the accident* and how much she loved and missed Craig." Eric shook his head. "The police finally found her not too long ago. She was dead, overdosed in a public park. A runner found her sprawled on a creek bank."

"And Sir?" Liam's voice was gruff.

"Haven't found him yet. But he'll pay," Eric whispered.

"Eric, you have to let the police handle it," Liam said. He understood Eric's motives and desire to see the man pay, but Liam didn't want to see the property manager arrested and spending the rest of his life suffering with his pain alone in jail.

"I've got it taken care of, it's all under control." Eric turned glazed eyes Liam's way. "It will all be over soon."

"I don't want to see you in trouble. You've been hurt enough."

"I'll gladly hurt every minute of every day until my last breath if it means vindication for Craig, for every victim of sexual assault. My pain is worth it if it brings them some peace." Eric jutted his jaw as if daring Liam to argue.

"I get it, I so get it." Liam struggled with his words. "And part of me agrees, appreciates it, and wants every victim to be given peace. But you need to protect yourself, keep yourself safe. You can honor Craig, keep his memory alive, help others find their peace. You don't have to do this."

Liam didn't *say* that he now almost one-hundred percent knew that Eric was the killer—maybe he still had a sliver of doubt—but he couldn't have been any clearer. His brain and heart were so torn. Liam wanted to join Eric and go on a crusade to vindicate all of the victims—people like himself who lived with the nightmares of their past, some their present—but he found himself swirling in a messy mixture of right and wrong. His former black and white view on the situation had suddenly been swamped in a thousand shades of gray and he didn't like it. *Right, wrong, black, white, good, bad*, Liam's head spun. He wanted offenders to be punished, to hurt, to suffer. But Liam also realized that the efforts Eric was putting into vindicating Craig and others were only going to eventually end with him in prison. Instead, Liam saw that energy going to help, to support, to fighting the fight and vindicating in a more positive way.

"It's too late for that." Eric shook his head. "I've got my own demons and now I've adopted Craig's demons. My head isn't right. I can't change things." He turned toward the back room. "I need to work. Please leave me alone."

Liam sighed and fought back tears. Tears for Craig, for all the other victims, for himself, *and* for Eric's pain.

When he slid back into his truck, unsure how he'd get through even a day at work let alone day after day, week after week, he saw several texts from Drake. With an aching heart, Liam ignored the texts and pointed his truck toward the site. He wasn't ready to talk to Drake. His head and heart were too jumbled, too painful, just too much right now. He *wanted* to let Drake hold him, tell him he loved him, *listen* to him. But Liam feared another fight, another cold, dismissive response to his concerns and fears. Drake was still deep in his work. He couldn't and wouldn't leave his job responsibilities for Liam—and Liam wouldn't ask him to. But maybe this was one of those times where the men were going to have to realize personal and professional had to stay separate—and the lines were just too blurred on this particular situation.

Liam would give himself and Drake some time.

Time to think, to reassess, to heal.

His heart hurt, but he hoped they could come together with a plan on how to stay in each other's lives without allowing their differing views to push them apart.

Is your view really all that much different than Drake's now?

Liam frowned as he sat in his truck, staring at the site and his men setting to work. *I mean, I still believe it's not a loss to have offenders show up dead.*

But?

I guess I can admit that murder isn't acceptable—even though it feels rewarding to think of those monsters suffering. Liam gripped the steering wheel. *And as much as I want that type of payback, I can see there are other ways to help, support, and fight for victims.*

Are those ways you'd be interested in looking into?

Liam scoffed, drained the rest of his now lukewarm coffee, and bolted from the truck. He wasn't in the headspace to let his mind go there just yet.

11

———

DRAKE

DRAKE PULLED up the collar of his light jacket. It was a flimsy attempt to block out the damn icy, wet wind, but who knew winter was going to battle like such a bitch as spring was *trying* to come to town. The day before, he'd admired the flowering trees. Today the biting wind seemed to be trying to take out any sign of spring. Drake shivered as he walked into the little café.

He'd been at work non-stop—before and after the shit show with Liam—and this day was no different. His coffee from the morning was a distant memory and he *had* to get out of the office to stretch his legs and clear his head before diving back into the quicksand of reports and paperwork and digging for answers.

He ordered two coffees—one extra hot for later—and a couple sandwiches and chips. He threw in a couple cookies, paid for his order, and took a step to the side to wait for his items to be prepared.

Drake pulled out his phone. It was pointless. He knew that. Liam wasn't answering his texts. But Drake held out hope. It had been a week and no response from Liam. Drake was torn—on one hand, he knew he'd been a complete ass and deserved whatever anger Liam had toward him; on the other hand, how was Drake supposed to apologize and make things right if Liam wouldn't speak to him? Drake had been wrong to lash out at Liam. Period. And damned if his heart didn't ache a little more each day with the thought that his fucking job and inability to see anything but black and white had possibly cost him the best damned thing that had ever happened to him.

Drake was pulled from his thoughts when his name was called. He forced himself to sit at a table to eat one of the sandwiches and drink his coffee—he was headed back to the office for hours and hours of work, he *had* to give his head a break. But as soon as he was finished, Drake gathered his remaining food and coffee and pushed the door open against the pounding wind. And rain. Great, rain was just what Drake needed.

He was cold and damp by the time he walked into his office.

Less than one minute later, Mathers stood at the doorway, sly smirk on his face, arms crossed over his chest. "Lewis, you look like shit. When you going to admit these are coming my way too?"

"Do you ever fucking work? Even cold cases need to be solved. Go do something productive," Drake growled.

Mathers chuckled. "You're going to let these cases kill you. Don't you have some pretty young thing begging you to come home?"

Drake rolled his eyes, too tired to even be angry about Mathers trying to bait him. "Fuck off."

Mathers laughed as he strolled down the hallway. Seriously, did the man ever do any actual work?

Drake tossed the sandwich in the tiny fridge, put the cookies in his drawer, and started on the extra hot coffee —which was at a perfect temperature for drinking thanks to his walk in the icy rain.

Something close to two hours later—Drake had lost all grasp of time—he found himself moving away from the reports and archives as he began a wild goose chase into old news stories regarding homicides. It wasn't the best plan, but it was what Drake's exhausted mind could handle at the moment. Maybe a break from what he knew would bring some clarity.

Like Alice down the rabbit hole, Drake dove in.

Several hours later—Drake seriously didn't understand how his brain could shut out everything and be so hyper-focused on one thing for so long—a niggling of curiosity broke into his scrolling and he pushed away from the computer, blinking and glancing around as if trying to reacquaint himself with where he was. When his stomach growled, Drake stood and stretched. After a quick trip to the restroom, he returned and grabbed his extra sandwich and a bottle of water. Forcing himself to chew and swallow, a drink after each bite, Drake knew the five minutes it took him to eat weren't enough of a break, but he tossed the trash and returned his attention to the story that had caught his attention.

A child's body had been found in Big Racoon Creek right on the line of Putnam and Parke counties not too many months ago. Drake's victims were adults, sex offenders, all living in Marion County. But something about the travesty of a child dying in a creek had caught

Drake's attention and wouldn't let go. He checked the time. It was way too late to call into either Putnam or Parke County sheriff's departments and hope to get anyone who could give him more details. Plus...

"Damn it, Lewis. Go home. I'm not going to have your mental breakdown on my conscience," Simms grumbled from the door, interrupting Drake's thoughts.

"You're still here," Drake pointed out and frowned.

"I'm the damn Lieutenant and I can be here whenever I want. Just so happens that I've been home, had dinner with my wife, went to my son's track meet, and came back here to check on you. You're done for the day. Go home."

Drake opened his mouth to argue. But the look on Simms' face shut him down. Not much more he could do right then. He'd get a good night's sleep and hit it hard again the next day. "Fine," Drake huffed. He stood and followed Simms out the door. "How was the track meet?"

"Cold as fucking hell," Simms griped. "Felt like damn winter out there. Track in decent temps is a lot more enjoyable."

Drake laughed. "I bet."

They walked toward the parking lot, their cars parked near each other.

"Get some sleep. Enjoy some time with whoever's waiting on you at home," Simms suggested. "Get back to it tomorrow."

"No one at home," Drake mumbled. *Because I ruined it and maybe lost Liam for good.*

"Thought you and that foreman, the lake house," Lieutenant Simms rambled and then clamped his mouth shut. "You know what, never mind. Who is or isn't at your place isn't my damned business. Go home, take a long hot shower, and get some sleep. I'd say take the morning off for good measure, but we both know that's not going to happen, so just get some sleep." The older man waved and climbed into his car.

Drake stared after Simms' car until the brake lights disappeared. He mulled over his lieutenant's words. Simms knew about Liam? Or at least suspected? Did anyone else? And Simms didn't seem bothered by it. Drake frowned, but a smile tugged at his lips. Maybe being out at work wouldn't be the worst thing ever.

Then Drake's heart caught in his chest. Without Liam, it wouldn't matter whether he was in the closet or out. Without Liam, Drake had no one—definitely no one worthy of coming out at work for. He climbed into his car and drove home with only two things on his mind. How—if anything—was the dead child related to his victims? The child was haunting his thoughts, almost as if trying to tell Drake something but he wasn't catching on.

And Liam. Drake blew out a long breath. After a shower, Drake would attempt to contact Liam again. He wanted so badly to fix what he'd messed up.

But could he? Could Drake fix how differently he and Liam saw things?

He wasn't sure. But he damned sure wasn't going to give up on Liam without a fight. That man had brought Drake the only happiness and fulfillment he'd ever had in his life. Drake wasn't ready or willing to give up on that.

He could only hope that Liam wasn't giving up either.

Drake had just enough energy for a shower while his frozen pizza baked. Tasting barely anything, and washing the food down with a bottle of water, Drake climbed into bed and grabbed his phone.

. . .

DRAKE: *Hey, heading to bed, but wanted to say good night and I love you. I really wish we could talk. I need to fix this, I was wrong and I'm sorry.*

DRAKE SCROLLED through some news stories on the off chance that Liam would reply. With each story, the hope he felt slipped further and further away. His chest ached with the reality of the fact that Drake had possibly lost Liam because of his job and his inability to empathize with the man.

More than anything, Drake wanted to let Liam know that he'd realized his steadfastness toward right and wrong, black and white, was not always the best way to approach a situation. Liam had given him the cold shoulder and plenty of time to think. Drake had never needed to see things differently in his line of work. A person broke the law, there were consequences. Period.

But in his personal life, dealing with a man he loved very much—and that was part of his problem, he didn't know how to deal with a relationship or loving someone—Drake had started to see how things weren't always one way or another, not always cut and dry. Relationships—loving someone—had room for a lot of gray area and Drake was learning that.

He scoffed at himself. For someone who was as good as he was at what he did for a living—and he honestly did have to be fairly smart to do his job, or at least to do his job well—he was pretty confident that he was a tad ignorant in the area of love.

And if you're honest with yourself, that ignorance—the not knowing how to handle a relationship when things didn't go exactly the way you needed them to—is what led you to react to Liam the way you did the other day. Sure, you were exhausted and stressed, but the unknown and newness of what you two have scared you.

Just as Drake was about to tell himself to fuck off and toss his phone to the side, it buzzed in his hand. With his heart in his throat, Drake scanned the screen.

LIAM: I love you, too. I do want to fix this, but I'm not 100% sure we can. I need more time to think things through and decide if we can work it out when we have such differing views. Get some sleep.

WITHOUT HESITATION, Drake tapped out a quick reply.

DRAKE: I'm learning how to accept those differing views. Figuring out how to shift my views about work and the law to something more personal when it comes to the man I love. I want to give it a chance, work together to fix it. I just need time to prove to you that I'm trying to see things in a different light.

DRAKE'S HEART was hopeful and his eyes droopy when Liam replied with *Give me some time. I love you and I'm interested in fixing things. I'm just not ready right this moment.*

. . .

DRAKE SMILED as he tapped out *I'll wait for you forever* before he drifted off to sleep.

The next day, Drake felt almost rested as he walked into his office with two coffees. One regular and one extra hot—again. They'd hopefully get him through until lunch.

He pulled up all of the notes and reports he'd been drowning in the day before and made a plan of attack for the day.

First on his list was to speak to whoever was in charge of the dead child's case. He started with the Putnam County sheriff, but quickly learned that the case was in Parke County.

By the time he hung up with the Parke County sheriff, Drake had a strange feeling in his gut that he didn't stumble across the news story about the kid on accident.

The sheriff, Dustin Shoal, had agreed to update Drake on the case. Shoal reported that the child had died of blunt force trauma, but it was unclear if he'd died before or after he was in the water. The child had also been sexually assaulted based on medical reports.

In the very beginning of the case, they'd struggled to name suspects, but the tiny department had eventually gotten names and set to work finding the suspects, digging into their backgrounds and whereabouts, and bringing them in if necessary. So far, all but one had been ruled out in the child's death. Shoal's biggest suspect was Billy "Buzz" Cotton, but he'd disappeared—*like a damn magic trick* Shoal had said. Likely back to Indianapolis, but Buzz was definitely laying low—Shoal had been in contact with all the proper departments in the county and city regarding the suspect. Drake assured Shoal that he'd help with the Parke County case if he could and set to finding out all he could about Billy "Buzz" Cotton. Drake usually wouldn't have involved himself in a case that wasn't assigned to him, but he had a feeling that it definitely had connections to his dead bodies so he dug in.

An hour later, Drake's stomach rolled and his teeth nearly broke off as he read through all of the reports he'd pulled on Buzz Cotton. The man was a menace to society and deserved to rot. From what Drake could find—having access to records was a definite perk—Billy had a long history of misdemeanor crimes. But he also had felony charges. And he had to be one of the luckiest pieces of shit on the planet because more than one of his charges and court hearings had been thrown out because of mess-ups and pure ineptitude. So Billy, a criminal of the worst kind—preying on innocent children—had done a lot of time behind bars, but he'd also walked in so many cases that Drake had trouble understanding just how the man had managed to continually get off with only a slap on the wrist. And every time that happened, Billy was free to go out and find more victims.

Drake vowed to continue looking for his murder suspect, but he had a niggling thought that just wouldn't go away about Billy and he swore he'd do what he could to help Shoal find the bastard and bring him in. Billy Cotton needed to pay for his crimes. All of them. And definitely for that little boy found in the creek.

From what Drake had heard from Shoal and read in the records, all they needed to do was *find* Billy. Making sure he was punished would be easy from that point based on the number of warrants out on him. But the man was a lifelong criminal, he knew what he was doing and was so far eluding the police very well.

Drake headed to talk to some of the officers he knew. He wanted to give them a head's up on Billy Cotton and make sure they knew to keep an eye out. Drake rolled his eyes. The officers would have already been briefed, but he felt better knowing he was giving them information as well.

Four days later, Drake's office phone rang.

"Lewis," he answered.

"Sheriff Shoal here. With help from Indianapolis, we brought in Buzz Cotton. Don't know where he got the money for such a big name attorney—likely drug money—but he spent a night in jail—which are sitting packed beyond capacity—and now he's released with an ankle bracelet and a court date." The sheriff sounded pissed that Cotton wasn't sitting in jail until his court appearance.

"So, he's back in Indy? Just an ankle bracelet? That's nothing for a piece of shit like Cotton," Drake growled.

"Agreed. I've talked to the guys who found him up there in Indy—brought him in for a busted tail light and disorderly conduct," Shoal chuckled. "They're going to run patrols on his house until his court appearance. The judge assigned a date that's coming up pretty soon, so hopefully he will stay put."

"I've looked at the guy's records. If history repeats itself, he'll get off on some mix-up or stupidity on the part of someone else. Wonder if it's the same attorney—if so, he's probably already working on how to get Cotton off even with all the other warrants and such." Drake blew out a frustrated breath. "Can you keep me updated? He's clearly not part of my cases since he's not dead and buried in concrete, but there's something about Cotton that's caught my attention and I want to see him brought to justice. For that little boy." *For that little boy. For all of the children. For Liam.*

As Drake and Sheriff Shoal said their goodbyes, a thought as powerful as a speeding freight train slammed into Drake and he nearly stopped breathing.

Could Billy "Buzz" Cotton have been one of the men who slapped Liam around? Could he have been *the* man who sexually assaulted Liam? Nausea rolled through Drake as he gasped for air. It was wrong, but he didn't give a fuck, he wanted to barge into the patrol captain's office, demand to know where Cotton was living under house arrest, and beat the monster within an inch of his life. For Liam, for all the children, all the women, all the people Buzz Cotton had hurt and destroyed.

Guess you're able to see a bit beyond that black and white, right and wrong now.

Drake chuckled humorlessly, longed for Liam to call him—he wanted Liam to come to him, to come *home*—and wearily dug back into the cases in front of him. He was so ready to be done with dead bodies showing up in concrete.

A WEEK LATER, Drake looked up at a knock on his office door.

"Lewis, we've got another body," Simms stated from the doorway. Arms crossed, frowning, the lieutenant looked as if he wanted to be *anywhere* but at Drake's door.

Drake stared at Simms for several seconds as he processed the information. His thoughts were like molasses through a sieve. "Fuuuck," he groaned.

"I'll send you what I've got. Not gonna sugar coat it. We need to get an arrest made. Four bodies, no suspects." Simms frowned. "The city is beyond concerned. The media is prepped and ready to begin dragging us through the mud. Wannabe crime solvers are filling up our phone lines with their hypotheticals and conjecture." The lieutenant ran a hand over his face. "I don't want you working yourself to death, but I need this done and over."

"You and me both," Drake grumbled. "Media could let the general public know that they're safe unless they're a sex offender," he mused.

"Yeah, gotta say, I can't see a lot of harm in monsters like that being picked off. If I had my way, we'd let this guy keep knocking them off and making our city a better place." Simms sighed.

Drake's eyes grew wide.

"But we've got laws to uphold and a killer to catch. Need to make it happen a lot sooner rather than later." Simms gave a nod.

Drake thought over what his superior had said—holy hell, even Simms could see that sex offenders dying wasn't necessarily a bad thing. Drake was beginning to think he was the only one who hadn't already learned to see gray area, even in a law enforcement position.

As he rubbed his temples and waited for the digital and physical documents Simms was sending, Drake's phone rang.

"Lewis," he growled.

"It's Shoal. Sorry, should've called sooner, but I've been swamped. Billy Cotton was supposed to show up at his court appearance two days ago, but the day before that, his ankle bracelet had a very convenient malfunction.

When patrol went to check on him, he was nowhere to be found. My men and my contacts in Indy are working on it, but Cotton is back on the loose. I figure he's going to go even further underground."

"Fuck," Drake snapped. "I'm up to my eyeballs in shit here, keep me updated." He disconnected and pulled up the reports Simms had sent.

A knock at the door brought a thick file folder delivered by one of the assistants. "Everything we've got on Billy Cotton, sir."

Drake took the folder as he remembered he'd asked for the physical records. "Thanks," he mumbled.

Drake had to get to the crime scene, but he also wanted to go through all of the information he'd been able to gather on Billy Cotton, on the child found dead in the creek, and on the other dead bodies. Between what Shoal was willing to send over, what Drake had been able to dig up, and the information readily available, Drake had hours and hours of combing through reports ahead of him.

He sighed. If he never had to stare at names and numbers and histories and incident reports ever again it would be way too soon.

Three hours later, Drake returned from the crime scene and stalked into his office, slamming the door behind him. He trusted his team to gather everything needed. He'd talked to witnesses. He'd talked to the man who found the body. It was found at a southside construction site. Not one Liam was associated with. Not even a Corsen Construction site. Not that Drake had ever truly suspected Liam, but he gave a little sigh of relief.

Dave Houston, however, wasn't out of the picture. Drake needed to know if he'd had any access to the concrete at the construction site. He had one of his team members looking into that.

The man who found the body—a foreman on the site— had been doing a check around the construction. "Checking the concrete to be sure it was ready for the next steps in building. When the crew helped me remove the forms, a section was bubbled and crumbly. I poked at it with a crowbar—honestly, probably harder than I should have. I was pissed it was going to set us back on our schedule because the whole thing was going to have to be torn up and re-poured." The foreman had huffed. "Guess it doesn't matter now since we're screwed on time for sure. Anyway, messed with it with the crowbar and saw the hand. After hearing the news of the other bodies in concrete lately, I didn't mess with it anymore. Called 911 right away."

Drake threw himself into his chair and picked up his phone. "Get me another monitor in here," he barked.

Thirty minutes later, Drake had three monitors set up, three piles of papers and folders, and a whiteboard hanging from his wall. A stack of sticky notes and a dry-erase marker in hand, Drake set to work.

He barely acknowledged the brown bag delivered two hours later, but he absentmindedly ate the food Simms had sent in while going back and forth between monitors, board, and folders.

Thanks to the pressure Lieutenant Simms had been able to apply, Drake got the big break he was looking for when the fourth body was identified.

Billy "Buzz" Cotton wouldn't be hurting children any more.

And Drake's heart gave a little thrill at that thought.

But Drake still hadn't made an arrest. He needed the killer brought in. Now.

It was well past midnight, Drake had been at work since six the previous morning. He quickly made a pile of records that didn't appear to be useful to him. He wasn't ready to send them back to records just yet, but most of what was in the folders was also available digitally.

With his office set up and prepared for him to dive right back in upon his return, Drake turned off the lights, locked his office door, and headed home. He needed a shower and sleep. He was so tired he couldn't even think of eating. He'd grab breakfast on the way back to the office in less than six hours.

With a quick check of his phone and no message from Liam, Drake showered and fell into a deep sleep. When the cases were over, he vowed to sleep for a week.

When his alarm went off at six that morning, Drake rolled from bed on autopilot. His brain begged for answers and his body begged for rest. Drake was determined to find the connection, the answer, the clue he was looking for. He needed these cases solved. He longed for a break. Drake promised himself, after he solved these cases—and if Liam would give him a chance to make things right—he'd slow down at work. He got paid the same despite how many cases he took on. He knew Simms would be on board with Drake cutting back on his cases from time to time.

Drake settled in at his desk with a bag of fast food breakfast and two large cups of coffee. "Need answers. Point me in the right direction. Let's go," Drake mumbled to himself as he dove into the information on his desk.

An hour later, one of the coffees empty, Drake froze

and forced himself to read and re-read the file in front of him.

The kid who was found in the creek was Craig Fischer. Mother was Crissy Fischer. She was involved with Billy Cotton shortly before and at the time of Craig's death. She disappeared and was later found dead, overdosed, in a park. Craig Fischer had been removed from Crissy's custody and placed in emergency foster care with an uncle, Crissy's brother.

Eric Cooper.

An Eric Cooper was the property manager at Shadow Woods.

It wasn't an uncommon name. Could it have been a coincidence?

Drake dug a bit further and connected the two. The uncle who had taken in Craig was the same Eric Cooper who managed Shadow Woods.

According to the report, Eric had petitioned the courts for adoption of Craig. Crissy had signed off on the first request, but later went back on it and said she wanted Craig back with her. The kid was eventually returned to his mother and shortly after, he was found dead in the creek with obvious sexual trauma.

A million-to-one said Billy Cotton assaulted the kid. Whether he meant to kill him or not would have died with Billy.

But Eric Cooper had a very clear motive to kill Billy Cotton. He actually had a motive to kill any and all sex offenders. Whether he went after specific offenders or randomly killed those he was able to find remained to be seen.

But Eric was a top suspect.

He was dangerous.

And Liam worked near Eric daily.

Fuck.

DRAKE: *Hey, got some new information on these cases. Need you to stay away from Eric Cooper. I think he's dangerous. Can you let me know you got this?*

12

LIAM

LIAM GLANCED up from the blueprints and groaned under his breath. Eric Cooper was beginning to be a pain in his ass. The man was likely lonely, he'd gone through a very painful family issue, he was grieving. Liam got all of that and did his best to understand.

But Eric kept just showing up at the site.

Kinda like you kept showing up at his office and butting into his personal life?

Liam sighed. He was used to curious bystanders stopping to watch the construction from time to time. But Eric pushed what was allowed and ended up in the way a lot of times. Okay, maybe not *in the way*, but definitely too close for Liam's comfort as far as safety was concerned.

And Eric had been weird recently.

Liam knew grief made people act differently, but Eric was running the gamut. Angry and biting off heads, jittery and anxious, way too calm and serene, sneaky and standoff-ish, the man was like an emotional ping-pong ball and Liam had trouble keeping track of which Eric would show up at any given time. He would be glad when they wrapped up their work at Shadow Woods and he could say goodbye to Eric Cooper.

Right. You'll just completely forget about the guy who you're pretty sure is killing sex offenders. You'll never think about the guy you have such high suspicions of that you're hiding them from your detective boyfriend. Mmhm.

The thought of Drake hit Liam square in the gut. He missed the man he loved. Liam wanted to talk to Drake, wanted to spend as many hours working things out as they needed, but he was also afraid their differing viewpoints—and Drake's inability to separate his job point of view from his personal life point of view—were too much and would keep them apart. As much as Liam wanted to see Drake and fix things, he worried that a second blowup shit show would be too much for him to take. Maybe a clean break was what they both needed.

Does it feel like a clean break? Does it feel like you'd be able to move on from him?

Liam sighed. No. He needed to talk to Drake.

But would Drake have time for him? Liam had been watching what he could of the news and didn't think there'd been any arrests in Drake's cases and the media was indicating a new body was likely related.

He walked to the cab of his truck and grabbed his phone, ready to text Drake. But he paused. It was smack dab in the middle of a work day. For both of them. He should wait until later. Get home, clear his head, and talk to Drake then.

A voice beside him made Liam jerk. "See? I'm being a good boy and staying away from the concrete," Eric stated in a somewhat manic sounding voice. "At least for now.

Maybe not later. But I got my reward so I'll be good for now."

What the hell was the man talking about?

"Yeah, stay away from the concrete. Actually, best if you just stay away from the site. It's a safety issue and I'd rather not get my ass nailed." Liam glanced at his phone one last time—no, he was making the right decision to wait before contacting Drake when they could both talk— and tossed it on the seat of his truck before giving Eric a slight wave and heading to speak to one of the heavy equipment operators.

Liam didn't like Eric hanging around—the man was definitely in one of his stranger-than-normal phases—but as property manager, Eric had the right to be on the property and he technically wasn't doing anything *wrong*. He was just rubbing Liam in the wrong way.

Which was weird. Liam felt nearly one hundred percent sure that Eric was killing sex offenders. While he felt no sorrow for their deaths, he began to wonder what would happen if Eric were allowed to keep on with no consequences. Would the man get more and more indiscriminate? Begin going after *family* of sex offenders? Public defenders or hired defense attorneys of sex offenders? Liam wasn't upset about sex offenders being rid from the earth, but he could see how it could quickly get out of hand. And, deep in his soul, he knew that killing another human was wrong. Liam didn't want to get Eric in trouble, but he knew he needed to tell Drake about Eric's past and about Liam's suspicions.

Would Eric end up serving multiple life sentences for the murders? Three dead bodies had shown up—shit, no, it was now four if the media reports had it right. Four bodies. Four life sentences? Or were there more bodies that hadn't been found?

Liam glanced back toward his truck and saw that Eric was *still* there. Arms crossed, eyes narrowed, Eric stared at Liam in such a way that Liam was a bit unnerved. He shook it off and went back to assisting the Bobcat operator.

Tonight. Tonight, Liam and Drake would talk. Liam would tell Drake about Eric. They'd work things out. He sighed inwardly—Liam had missed being in Drake's arms and now all he could look forward to was returning to Drake, to *home*, because wherever Drake was, was exactly where Liam wanted to be. Forever and always.

Several hours later, Liam sighed. He was grateful that the day had been extremely busy, it made the time go by faster. He'd sent all his men home once they'd finished the necessary steps in closing down a site for the night. Liam wanted to do one last walk-through and then he'd head home.

As he walked toward his truck, Liam noticed a shadow in the dusky darkness. Damned Eric. "Hey, man, gotta go so I can check off on the site being secure for the night."

Eric laughed. "Yeah, because you checking it as *secure* completely makes it so that no one can get in. Mess with the machines. Fuck up the concrete."

Liam narrowed his eyes at Eric who seemed to be the most unstable Liam had ever seen him. "Come on, I'm tired. Want to get home. I'll see you tomorrow."

"You know, I was out here just minding my own business, watching the progress on *my* property and trying to clear my head." Eric frowned and stared off into the distance. "Do you know how painfully full of bad shit my head gets these days?" He shook his head as if breaking from a completely different train of thought. "Anyway, out here doing no one any harm—which is kinda ironic if you give it enough thought," Eric chuckled, but it wasn't a laugh of someone who really thought something was funny. "And then I see a most unfortunate bit of information."

Liam crossed his arms over his chest and cocked his head, not in the mood for games. "And what was that?"

"Well, you tossed your phone down with no care as to privacy so I couldn't help but read the text that came through from your detective boyfriend. Drake thinks I'm dangerous and wants you to stay away from me. I'm surprised it took him so long to figure it out—you pegged me a lot sooner than he did. Yet you didn't tell him. Why is that?" Eric cocked his head. "Ahh, you were hurt too. You're like me. The pain is so bad that you welcome the relief of knowing one more pedophile is off the streets. So, you let me be, let me keep going, let me do the dirty work of killing every piece of shit sex offender."

"Look, I really want to get home," Liam began, his heart thudding in his chest now that Eric knew that both Liam and Drake suspected him. "While I'm somewhat torn, I have to say that I think you need to turn yourself in. If Drake has figured you out, it won't be long before he comes for you. He's likely on his way." Oh God, Liam hoped that Drake was on his way and had everything lined up to take Eric in. "Maybe you can avoid some punishment if you turn yourself in and cooperate. But you have to stop killing sex offenders."

Liam turned to get into his truck. He'd drive off and hope that Eric got bored and returned to his apartment.

But just as Liam put a leg into the cab, a hand came around to cover his face. He grunted in surprise and his nose filled with a sweet chemically scent.

"Shhh, it's okay," Eric whispered as Liam fought against him. "You've become a liability. You should have just let it go, let me go. You know how much those monsters hurt others, you should have let me keep easing pain and bringing them to justice. But now you've forced my hand."

Liam's world shifted as a wave of dizziness washed through him. When a painful thud sounded against his head, Liam wondered for a brief second what Eric had hit him with and then his world went black.

When Liam came to, he knew immediately that he wasn't at the construction site. He was inside. The floor was cold and rough. Probably concrete. He shifted and pain shot through his head. Blinking against the dizziness, Liam kept his eyes mostly closed as he attempted to take in his surroundings.

He was slumped on the floor, a wall against his back, one single battery-powered lantern gave off a dim light, and a garage type door was closed in front of him. Liam gathered he was in a storage unit. The question was, *which* storage unit? Near Shadow Woods? Even if he knew that, there were likely at least ten to twenty units on the near southside. Would anyone know he was missing? He'd been pretty much on radio silence with Drake since their argument and Drake was up to his eyeballs in his cases. Would he even realize Liam was missing?

Liam's head was throbbing and he fought dizziness and nausea, likely all from the chloroform and the bump to his head. Where was Eric? How long had it been since they left the construction site? Did Eric drive Liam's truck? How did Eric drag Liam from the truck into the storage unit? How long had Liam been on the floor? Based on how stiff and sore he was, Liam guessed it had been at least a few hours.

He risked a tiny movement to glance around. If Eric was gone, Liam had a decent chance of getting out of the unit. When he saw he was alone, Liam blew out a sigh of relief and gingerly sat up. His head pounded, but after a few moments, he was able to move past the pain. Reaching to his back pocket, with very little hope of finding his phone, Liam cursed when he felt empty pockets. That meant his phone was either in the truck, with Eric, or destroyed.

Liam stood slowly. With luck, his truck would be outside. With more luck, the keys would be available. He'd never learned how to hotwire a car, so he was screwed with no keys. If needed, he'd take off on foot and find a phone.

As Liam approached the rolling door, he realized with a huff at his own stupidity that it was likely locked from the outside. "Fuck, you idiot."

A clinking sound caught Liam's attention right before the door rolled up with a clang and clatter. Liam wasn't sure who was more shocked, him or Eric. But Eric stepped inside and swung a long metal pipe toward Liam's head.

Liam stepped back, landed wrong on his ankle, and fell to the ground. His ankle hurt, but he'd avoided the pipe to the head. "Fuck, man. Is that what you hit me with earlier? Left a damn huge bump and pain," Liam grumbled as he rubbed the goose egg on the side of his head, hoping Eric was in one of his friendlier moods.

"Why couldn't you keep your nose out of my business?" Eric muttered. "I wasn't hurting you. I wasn't hurting anyone who didn't deserve it. Then you had to step in and start figuring things out. And your damned self-righteous prick of a boyfriend had to save the world." He ran a hand over his face as he paced. "I was getting rid of evil. You could have just let it go."

"I didn't turn you in," Liam stated in hopes of keeping Eric calm and giving himself more time. Time for what, he wasn't sure. Liam wanted to believe that Drake would be looking for him, but he knew it was a long shot. Maybe his best hope was for Drake to be looking for Eric and find Liam by association.

"Maybe not, but now you're a liability. And Lewis is on to me. It's only a matter of time. I needed more time, I had more targets, but I got the main one," Eric rambled.

"Who was the main one?" Liam decided his best option was to keep Eric talking.

"I got him. I got that prick who hurt Craig. I got him good. Made him suffer." Eric had a gleam in his eyes. "It was the only way to make it right. He had to die. An eye for an eye. He hurt Craig and killed him. I hurt him and killed him."

"How did you know who to go after?" Liam had truly wondered if Eric was targeting specifics or just randoms.

"I only killed sex offenders with crimes against children. Figured there was a good chance I'd get him if I just kept knocking them off." Eric waved his arm in a wild gesture. "Lucked out that I found him so quickly, but there are so many more who need to pay."

"How'd you get so lucky?" Liam asked.

"I keep track of sex offenders on that public site. They

have to register, you know? So, I'd found Billy Cotton.
Didn't realize who he was, just knew he needed to die.
Kept an eye on him. Noticed the police were tracking him
too. Knew something was up. Heard some asshole friend
of his refer to him as *Sir* and that's what the prick always
made Craig call him. Knew then I had my grand prize. So,
when Billy took a trip to the grocery, I hid in his backseat.
Jammed a knife in his side when he got back in the car."
Eric chuckled. The eerie sound made Liam shiver. "He
squealed like a stuck pig. Started pleading for his life and
said the police would be there soon if he didn't get right
home because of the ankle bracelet. I had some fun with
him, made him drive toward his house and then I cut it off
and threw it in his front yard. Figured that bought me
some time. Made him drive to a secluded area. Tortured
him and made him beg for his life. Made sure he knew
everything I did was in the name of all of his victims.
Killed him. Then cut him up and put him in the concrete."

"Craig wouldn't want you in trouble for him. Killing
won't bring him back," Liam whispered.

"Don't you want that pain to end?" Eric asked. "Every
monster I kill is one less who can hurt kids. Kids like
Craig. Kids like you." Eric's voice broke and Liam
recognized the man was about to lose it.

Liam had to keep him calm and talking. "Why
concrete? How did you find the places that had fresh
concrete?"

Eric smiled. "I'm good at keeping my eyes and ears
open. The police haven't even found all of them. Some of
the bodies I had more time to bury. Some were rush jobs.
But it's not hard to find where concrete is going to be
poured if you just pay attention. It's always best to get the

pieces in and secured first if possible. But if not, you can just shove them in and they'll usually stay put." He laughed. "Not like they were going anywhere." He pursed his lips. "I kept them out here until I could find the right spot. I'd take them to the locations in pieces, couldn't exactly lug around a whole dead body." Eric giggled almost hysterically.

"Out here? Where's out here?" Liam realized that maybe he wasn't at a storage facility.

"Don't worry about it. You're not going to need to know." Eric turned to stare at Liam. "You shouldn't have gotten involved. Now you have to be taken care of. I don't want to hurt you, but you asked for it with your nosy questions. May have to take out Detective Lewis too." Eric got a far-away look in his eyes. "Yeah, that's what I'll do. Get Lewis out here, kill you both, then move on. I can start up anywhere else. Go over to Ohio, set up a new name, start hunting for their monsters. I'll keep on until there's no breath left in me. I'll die before I rot in prison; why should I be punished and locked up when they're out and free to keep hurting children?"

Liam shook his head. For someone as clearly unstable as Eric was, Liam could definitely see his argument. "I don't know," he whispered. "But look, don't kill Drake. Kill me if you need to, but leave him out of this. You can start over in another state and not add killing a law enforcement agent to your crimes. Hell, you can walk away from here right now. Lock me in and leave. Get a head start and leave the state." Liam was near begging by that point, but he was feeling a lot more than a little fear.

"Shut up!" Eric lashed out. "You don't get to tell me what to do. This situation is your fault. I'll deal with it the way I want." He yanked Liam's phone from his back pocket. "Share your location with Drake."

Liam tried desperately to think of a way out, to think of a way to not involve Drake. But he knew Drake would eventually find Eric one way or an another. Maybe Liam and Drake together could overpower Eric. If Liam didn't do what Eric asked, the man would likely kill him and share the location either way. Best to keep Eric on whatever *good* side might be available and just do as asked.

Liam thumbed his phone, shared his location, and jumped when Eric jerked the phone out of his hand.

"And now we wait," Eric declared with an eerie glint to his eyes.

13

DRAKE

He kept at the reports and evidence files for several hours after texting Liam, but he couldn't focus. Liam hadn't replied and it was eating at Drake. Part of him wanted to give up, drive to Shadow Woods, and drag Liam away. But Drake needed the facts gathered in order to go after Eric Cooper. He had a job to do, just like Liam had a job to do. They were grown men with responsibilities and Drake needed to chill the fuck out. Just because Liam hadn't replied—not even once in several hours—wasn't necessarily bad news. Liam was likely busy. Maybe he was still upset. There were a lot of valid reasons for the unanswered text.

Yeah, like the fact you were a total ass to him not too long ago and he has a right to still be angry and hurt and not answering your text.

Drake growled. There were also a lot of *bad* reasons for Liam not answering the text. If Liam didn't know Eric Cooper, wasn't working right near him, then maybe Drake wouldn't be so worried.

Relax. Cooper has been killing sex offenders—if he's even the right guy—he'd have no reason to harm Liam.

Drake wanted to believe that. But his gut feeling told him something was off. Drake was a man who worked with facts and evidence, but there was something to be said for trusting when something felt wrong.

He grabbed his phone and called Liam. No answer. Even that wasn't entirely abnormal; Liam's phone may have been in his truck. But Drake took it as a sign that his instincts were on-point and decided something had to be done.

Drake needed to nab Eric Cooper, solve the murders, close the cases.

But more than anything, he needed to assure Liam's safety and fix things with the man he loved more than life.

Drake sat down at his desk and thought through his next move very carefully. He weighed pros and cons, contemplated anticipated actions, and made his decision. Drake knew he needed the force of the department behind him to be sure Cooper's arrest was done by the book and charges would stick. He would go to Simms with every bit of evidence he had gathered and make his case for Eric Cooper being brought in. He didn't think Simms would balk at that. But Drake also planned to tell Simms his concern that Liam was possibly in trouble.

That meant admitting he was gay and involved with Liam.

But that wasn't what was bothering Drake.

He anticipated Simms would remove him from the case. Temporarily or permanently, Drake couldn't guess. But having his boyfriend in a possibly dangerous situation with the suspect was definitely grounds for removal from actively pursuing an arrest.

With that prediction, Drake planned for something he never in his life thought he'd do. He copied, duplicated, and gathered everything he could find on Eric Cooper, stuffed it in his bag or saved it to his personal laptop, and prepared to go rogue. If Simms took him off the case— even if just until Liam was found—Drake certainly wasn't going to sit around and twiddle his damn thumbs until he was allowed back.

Oh, how the mighty has fallen. From black and white, right and wrong, cut and dry, by-the-book Detective Lewis to a man who is willing to risk his career to find his boyfriend.

Drake took a moment to consider that thought. It was accurate. He'd give up his job if it meant assuring Liam was safe.

What if Liam is safe but doesn't want to be with you? Is this just a last-ditch effort to prove to him that you can play in the gray area?

Drake frowned. He wanted Liam safe, no matter what. He'd think about their relationship status later.

With a last check that he had everything he might need to find Cooper—and something told him that if he found Cooper, he'd find Liam—Drake gave his office one last look, locked the door, and headed to fill Simms in on what he'd found.

He knocked on the lieutenant's office door frame and smiled when Simms gestured for him to enter the open door.

"Lewis, what do you have?" Simms finished typing something before turning his full attention to Drake.

Drake swallowed thickly when he noticed three other

people in the office. Mathers and two sergeants. *Out of the frying pan and into the fire,* Drake mused to himself. Getting Cooper and making sure Liam was safe was more important to Drake than his position in the closet when it came to work people knowing his business. But *damn*, why did it have to be fucking Mathers?

"Am I interrupting?" Drake nodded toward the other people in the room.

"No, not at all. We're waiting for one more to join an impromptu meeting." Simms waved him off. "Go ahead."

"I've got a suspect," Drake stated.

"You still thinking Dave Houston, the concrete guy?" Simms asked.

"No, sir. I've done enough digging to find out that Dave's alibi is pretty tight. His wife recently had a baby. Mrs. Houston has been having some significant postpartum depression and Dave had valid reasons for those shift switches." Drake paused. "I think we need to bring in the Shadow Woods property manager."

"That Cooper guy?" Simms asked.

Drake nodded.

With Simms immediately interested, Drake launched into history, reports, facts, evidence, *everything* he had on the dead bodies and Eric Cooper. Within moments, Drake knew he was preaching to the choir and Simms was completely on board with bringing in Cooper.

"Sir, I need to explain something. It's regarding my personal life, but despite my best efforts the two have merged and now I find myself needing to find Cooper for more reasons than just to bring him in on murder charges."

Simms brows arched and he waited patiently.

Pretending that the other three weren't in the room, Drake took a deep breath, imagined Liam taking his hand and urging him on, and spilled his guts. "Liam Walters is the foreman on the Shadow Woods construction project. I knew him in the past and we obviously met again with the first body found." Drake wanted to run from the room, but he recalled that Simms already suspected he and Liam were a couple. He imagined a life without Liam—a life where he could never be himself and enjoy something outside of his daily grind—and huffed a breath. "Liam and I are dating—he's my boyfriend," Drake rushed out.

Simms frowned and Drake caught the combined surprised and smiling faces of Mathers and the sergeants. He couldn't decipher if Mathers was more shocked or more pleased. And if he was pleased, was it a positive or negative reaction?

"Lewis, I don't give a damn who you date or spend your time with. How the hell does Liam Walters have anything to do with Eric Cooper?" Simms crossed his arms over his chest and leaned back in his chair.

Oh right, that.

Drake took another deep breath. "I think Cooper has Liam. I want to go after Cooper, but I'm also looking for Liam."

"What makes you think Liam is with Cooper?" Simms scowled.

"He's not answering texts, not answering his phone, and more than anything, my gut tells me something is wrong."

"Son, some unanswered texts and calls do not automatically mean that your boyfriend has been abducted by a suspected killer," Simms stated patiently.

"I'm aware of that. But I'm also aware that Eric is at the Shadow Woods construction site where Liam spends most of his days. Cooper has killed at least four men—although I'd venture to guess it's more than that—and isn't stable," Drake explained.

"How do you know that? Are you personally acquainted with Cooper?" Mathers interrupted.

Drake turned narrowed, impatient eyes toward Mathers. "If he's our killer—as in *murdering* people—he's clearly unstable. Murderers might not always be visibly unstable, but if he's taking the lives of others—even if he's killing sex offenders who deserve to suffer—he's not stable. If he's snapped and has Liam with him, I'm worried what he may do."

"So, you really going after Cooper or is this just a ruse to get the department to find your boyfriend?" Mathers kept on.

"I want the suspect brought in, the murders solved, the cases closed, and a civilian out of danger. Period."

"You've certainly presented enough evidence for me on Cooper. Liam involved or not, I want Eric Cooper brought in." Simms paused and studied Drake for a moment.

Here it is. The moment of truth.

"Lewis, I'm removing you from the case at least until Cooper is in custody," Simms stated and the glint in his eyes spoke of readiness for a challenge.

"I'd like to ask you to reconsider." Drake spoke calmly, but deep inside he was already making his next move.

"You're back on once Cooper is off the streets and Liam is found." Simms words left no room for argument.

"And if Liam isn't with Cooper?" Drake didn't want to think of that situation.

"Let's worry about getting Cooper in here first."

Drake realized with a start—although, he really wasn't surprised—that Simms trusted Drake's gut feeling on Cooper having Liam. "Can I ask to be updated on the case?"

"You're just giving up that easy?" Mathers questioned with narrowed, suspicious eyes.

Drake shrugged. "The sooner I step back, the sooner others can be brought up-to-speed and Cooper can be found." He turned toward Simms. "I'll keep trying to reach Liam. Could I take a bit to recoup at home?"

Simms nodded. "Probably for the best. We'll be in touch."

Drake pressed his lips together, hefted his laptop bag—which he worried had a neon sign indicating all the information Drake had taken with him—and gave a quick nod to everyone in the room before walking out with a breath held so tight he worried he'd pass out.

All he had to do was get home, dig into the information he'd borrowed—he liked that term better than stolen...holy shit, who was he and where was straight-as-an-arrow Drake Lewis? Anyway, he'd dive head-first into Cooper and figure out where to start looking.

Drake climbed into his car and, without much thought, took a couple side trips before heading home. Liam's truck wasn't at his place. It also wasn't at Shadow Woods. Eric's vehicle was at his apartment, but there was no answer when Drake knocked.

Wanting to be thorough before setting out on his pursuit to find Cooper, Drake went into the apartment complex office.

"Hi, can I help you?" a teenage girl asked but barely glanced up from her phone.

"Do you work here?"

"A couple hours here and there if Mr. Cooper isn't around."

"So, Mr. Cooper isn't here?" Drake asked.

She gave him a *duh* look.

"My bad, thought I saw his car."

She shrugged. "Don't know where he is. He went to watch the construction—he's so weird with wanting to watch concrete be poured—and hasn't come back."

Drake threw a glance over his shoulder. "Huh, thought they'd be done or at least wrapping the construction up for the day by now."

The girl popped her gum. "Yeah, saw most of them leave. Even the hottie boss man left. No clue where Mr. Cooper is."

Drake bit back a smirk. "You saw the hottie boss man leave?"

She nodded. "I watch for his truck every day."

"And he was driving?" Drake pressed.

"Don't know. I was doing some paperwork with a new renter. Saw the truck, would assume he was driving. Who else?"

Drake nodded. Who else, indeed. "Okay, thanks. Can you give me a call if Cooper shows back up?" He handed the girl his card.

"You wanting to rent a place? I can start the papers." She narrowed her eyes and looked at the card. "Detective? Holy shit, are you here because of that body they found? That was creepy as hell."

"Just let me know if you see Cooper *or* the hottie boss

man." Drake smiled and gave her a wink. He couldn't disagree with her assessment of Liam.

The girl blushed and nodded.

With that over, Drake drove home and unloaded every bit of information he'd been able to gather on Eric Cooper.

Three hours later, Drake nearly flipped his dining room table when he found the first bit of a possible clue as far as where Cooper may have been. The Cooper family had a large piece of land, definitely an out in the middle of nowhere type place, and Drake's heart thumped wildly as he scanned through dates and addresses and whatnot regarding the land.

From what he could find, the Cooper parents had died, but the land still showed up as Cooper-owned. Drake shoved his work phone in the inner pocket of his jacket in hopes of keeping it hidden. It had a tracker on it and Drake assumed the department would use it to search for him if he ended up missing. After sliding his wallet and personal phone into his pockets, Drake slipped a knife in his sock and his smallest handgun into the back waistband of his jeans.

Within forty-five minutes, Drake had reached the edge of Cooper's land. A house, barn, shed, and garage all sprawled at the top of a hill. But Drake knew there were also several miles of hills, woods, open fields, and creeks on the property. He maneuvered his car behind a thicket of brush and killed the engine. With his eyes closed and several deep breaths, Drake contemplated where he wanted to start searching. The department would do the exact same digging into Cooper as Drake had done, so it wouldn't be long before they arrived, too. They'd have more manpower for searching the wide expansive spaces, so maybe Drake should start at the buildings. But he was only one person, no backup, no law to support him, and he didn't want to risk starting in the house or garage only to have Cooper see him and flee. Or worse, go off the deep end and harm Liam.

If Liam was even with Eric.

And if Eric hadn't already harmed Liam.

His phone vibrated and a shiver of dread raced through him.

Liam Walters is sharing location.

Drake read and re-read the message several times.

Why would Liam share his location? Was this a random coincidence? Was Liam reaching out as a sign of wanting to fix things? Or was Drake's gut right and Liam was with Cooper against his will? If so, did Liam sneak the chance to share his location? Or was it a trap set up by Cooper?

Drake took a deep breath and blew it out slowly.

After running through several scenarios, Drake decided it was safest to assume the shared location was a ruse to get Drake to come for Liam. What Cooper wanted with Drake wasn't clear.

Really? Not clear? Not sure it could be any clearer. Usually isn't a good sign to be summoned by the murder suspect you've been working to arrest.

Either way, Drake checked his weapons and climbed out of the car. Grateful for the waning light, he zipped his jacket against the cold, damp air and set out to sneak toward the buildings while watching Liam's location on his phone. He cursed several times as he stopped to hide behind trees and wait for the location to update. The reception that far out was complete shit. But Drake at least knew the general location so even if the dot wasn't one hundred percent accurate, he knew he was heading in the right direction.

Unless it's just Liam's phone and not Liam.

Drake pushed aside the thought and focused on slowly making his way toward the barn and shed. Those appeared to be the closest to where Liam's location was. He'd start there and move on depending on what he found.

With a quick glance around in the dusky darkness, Drake sprinted toward the barn. The structure was old and in need of a lot of repair. Due to it being almost completely open and completely empty, Drake was able to make a quick sweep and declare the barn clear. No sign of struggle, no sign of anything other than dirt, hay, and dust.

He slipped from the barn, keeping to the shadows, and glanced left and right. Left and farther away was the garage. Right and closest to him was the shed type building. Similar to the garage in shape and rolling door, the shed was much smaller. Likely for a mower or similar.

Drake hunkered down and ran between the barn and shed. As he rounded the shed, plastered to the wall, he noticed a window. Creeping toward it, rising on his toes, Drake snuck a peek into the small building.

Liam.

Drake's heart clawed its way toward his throat.

Liam was inside. And alive.

The click of a gun exploded in Drake's head and pulled him from his celebration.

Fuck. He'd lost his focus and missed Cooper coming up behind him.

"Evening, Detective Lewis," Eric drawled. "So nice of you to join us. Won't you please come in?"

Drake gritted his teeth and held his hands up as Eric jammed the gun against Drake's head. As he walked toward the rolling door, Drake gathered his thoughts the best he could with a gun pointed at his head. Best case scenario, he and Liam could keep Cooper talking until the department got here. Or maybe they could overpower Eric. Worst case scenario, Eric snapped and killed one or both of them before the police arrived. Or after. Either way, he and Liam would be dead.

Drake swallowed thickly and pushed that thought away as he stepped into the shed. He nearly fell to his knees at the sight of Liam. His head had a bloody bump at the temple, he looked haggard, and he was favoring his ankle, but Drake swore no one had ever looked better in his whole life.

"I'm sorry," Liam blurted and threw himself into Drake's arms.

Eric kept the gun on Drake as they hugged, but soon cleared his throat. "Okay, that's enough. I didn't bring you here for a damn honeymoon."

Liam stepped back, but Drake grabbed his hand.

"Both of you, go sit down." Eric began to pace and gestured wildly toward the back of the shed. "Backs against the wall."

"Are you okay?" Drake whispered to Liam as they sat down.

"Yeah, just some bumps and bruises. God, I'm so glad you're here. I love you." Liam squeezed his hand. "You have a plan?" Liam's words were so quiet that Drake nearly missed them.

"Nothing great," Drake answered before turning his attention to the madman with the gun. Drake knew he *could* likely get to his gun and shoot Eric. But unless he had a perfect shot, Drake would likely only injure the man. And an injured man with a gun was just as dangerous. "Eric, the police are on their way. You need to turn yourself in. Don't add hostages to your list of offenses." He kept his words soft and as non-threatening as he could.

"Shut up!" Eric whirled around, gun waving. "You just shut up! You are the reason this is happening. Liam here was going to keep quiet. He suspected me *long* before you caught on."

Liam huffed. "I'm sorry. I wasn't sure and I was angry. I should have told you."

"It's okay," Drake whispered as Eric continued to rant and rave.

"Why couldn't you both just let this one go?" Eric's words were desperate. "Still could. Just let me keep doing good. Those bastards didn't deserve to live. They *hurt* those kids. Why should they get to go free—or even live in the comforts of jail—when so many of their victims' lives are ruined or cut short?"

Drake had no words and didn't think an argument on the subtleties of right and wrong in this situation would get him very far. The wild gleam in Cooper's eyes worried Drake. He feared Eric was going to snap which would likely end with Liam and Drake dead or Cooper escaping. And as much as Drake wanted to have Liam home and safe, he also wanted Eric brought in so the murder cases could no longer hang over Drake's head.

"Your goal is to kill sex offenders, get them off our streets, save their victims. You're not a murderer, you wouldn't want to kill innocent people. That's what Liam and I are. We've never preyed on children." Drake glanced toward Liam in question and got a hand squeeze in answer. "Liam suffered at the hands of one of those monsters. Why would you want to hurt him?"

Eric's face contorted in pain. "If you'd just left well-enough alone, none of this would have happened. I wasn't hurting anyone who didn't deserve it."

Now wasn't the time to point out to Eric all the havoc his killing spree had brought.

Cooper stared at Liam. "Maybe death is a relief. I often wonder if Craig was glad to die just to escape Billy Cotton and the pain he suffered at the hands of that man."

"I don't want to die, Eric," Liam spoke quietly. "I want to help other victims. I used to hide my painful past, but I've learned that a way to combat it is to reach out and support others. I don't know exactly what I'm going to do, but I'm going to help. I can't do that if you kill me."

"Maybe you should have thought of that before messing up my life!" Eric screeched.

Drake interrupted in hopes of steering the conversation back to a calmer side. "Is this your family's land?"

Eric, distracted by the question, blinked a couple times and nodded. "Yeah. Been in our family forever. Used to bring Craig here to play. He loved the creek and taking hikes through the woods. We'd hunt for morel mushrooms."

"Why did you bury the bodies in concrete? Why not bring them here?" Drake had often wondered about the concrete. Seeing the land Eric had available to him made Drake question the placement of bodies even more.

"I'd never disgrace this property or dirty this land with those monsters. Dead or alive, they didn't deserve a place like this, didn't deserve beauty or comfort." Eric's eyes shone with tears. "I wouldn't disrespect my family or Craig's memory by bringing them here."

An arc of light traveled through the small window and across the shed wall. Eric smiled an eerie smile. "Oh look, your crew has arrived. I don't want to kill you, I don't want to kill them. I want to leave here, never look back, start over. But I'll do what I have to do. I won't rot in prison when so many sex offenders are free and hurting children." He glanced toward Drake and Liam. "Don't move. I'm locking the door. If you're lucky, I'll be gone before they come for you."

Eric threw the rolling door up, walked out, slammed it closed, and applied the padlock.

Drake and Liam were left in silence.

"Thank you, I'm so sorry, I love you," Liam's words spilled from him as he threw his arms around Drake and held tight.

"Nothing to apologize for. I understand why you didn't tell me about Eric. To be honest, I likely wouldn't have taken it seriously—not sure you've realized but I'm a bit of an ass at times. I'm so sorry for the words I said. I didn't mean any of them. I clearly need to learn how to better handle exhaustion and stress." Drake tipped Liam's chin and feathered a kiss across his lips before brushing a finger over Liam's temple. "How bad is it?"

Liam closed his eyes and sighed. "God, I've missed you. It's not bad. Dull headache, but not terrible. I think the chloroform was worse than the head wound."

"He used chloroform? Damn, I'm sorry. I hear that stuff brings on a terrible headache." Drake shook his head. "I really don't think he's stable."

"Oh, he's unstable as a two-legged table and he's getting worse by the minute." Liam scowled. "If they take him in—and honestly, I think he'll kill himself before that happens—I worry what he'll do in custody. He doesn't want to be locked up, he's unstable, he's in a major depression over losing his nephew."

"They'll get him counseling and keep an eye on him," Drake assured.

"I guess I can sort of see, when faced with the two unbearable options, why he'd choose the one over the other." Liam leaned heavily against Drake.

"So, officially, I'm off the case. Simms removed me. I shouldn't be here." Drake smirked. "Probably should wait a bit before trying get out. Let the dust settle out there."

Liam's eyes went wide. "Are you going to get in trouble?"

Drake shrugged. "Maybe? Probably not. At least not too much. Simms may force me to take a couple weeks off."

"That doesn't sound like much of a punishment," Liam teased.

"Before you? It would have likely killed me. But now? It sounds like a dream come true. What do you think— even if Simms doesn't force me to take the time—want to spend two weeks at the lake house?" Drake raised his brows.

"When can we leave?" Liam asked and sighed heavily. "I'm ready for a break for sure."

Drake pulled him close and kissed the top of his head.

A single gunshot rang out in the silence.

"Shit," Drake mumbled.

"Can you tell who shot that?" Liam whispered.

"No, but the guys would be trying everything in their power to take him in and would only shoot if fired upon. With only one shot, I'd guess it was Cooper." Drake grimaced. "I'm sorry."

Liam shook his head. "It's not a surprise. The whole situation is just sad and painful for all involved."

A rattle sounded outside of the shed door followed by a clink and the door rolled up.

Drake reached for his gun, but stopped when he saw who was standing in the doorway.

Fucking Mathers.

Smiling wickedly.

Drake groaned. "What the fuck are you doing here?"

"Is that any way to speak to your rescuer?" Mathers stepped inside. "Simms let me tag along. I told him there was no way you were giving up that easy when he benched you. While they were digging into Eric Cooper, I pulled the tracking on your department phone. Sure enough, led us right to you. Cooper is dead, self-inflicted."

Drake nodded as he and Liam stood up.

"Any injuries? Need to call a unit out?" Mathers asked.

"Nah, since I'm off the case, I'll take Liam to the ER. Get him stitched up, check his ankle." Drake folded his arms over his chest. "Thanks for the assist. Appreciate it." And he did. Just why did it have to come from Mathers?

"You're too good of a detective to just walk away. I

knew that." Mathers shrugged. "We may rub each other the wrong way, but I'd expect the same from you. I respect your work."

"Does this mean you'll stop being a daily annoyance?" Drake cocked his head.

"Probably not," Mathers quipped with a chuckle. "Gotta keep you on your toes. Of course, who knows if you've got a job to come back to."

Liam's wide eyes traveled between Mathers and Drake.

"You know Simms isn't canning me. Maybe a forced vacation." Drake took Liam's hand. "Liam, this pain in the ass—who I now unfortunately owe big time—is Sam Mathers. Mathers, this is my boyfriend, Liam Walters."

Liam shook Sam's hand. "Nice to meet you. He may be a grumpy ass, but I'm *very* grateful for the rescue."

Mathers narrowed his eyes at Drake. "Sorry for all the shit I gave you about being gay. I didn't know. Was wrong either way." He smirked. "I'll just have to find something new to rib you about. Maybe your age? I think I may see some gray hair."

Drake groaned. "Let's get out of here. I need a vacation from *you*."

They walked the perimeter of the property toward Drake's car. He purposely didn't want Liam to see Cooper's body. And he didn't think Simms needed to see him at that exact moment.

Drake turned to Mathers as they reached the thicket. "Can you let Simms know that Liam and I will both be in tomorrow to answer any questions and do any paperwork? I want to get him to the hospital now."

"Sure thing." Mathers nodded. "And we'll get Liam's

truck processed and returned since Cooper drove it and all. I'll encourage the process to go as quickly as possible."

When Mathers was gone, Drake yanked Liam into a full-body hug and just held the man for several moments.

"You good?" Drake whispered.

"Yeah, I really am. Maybe it will hit me later, but I didn't feel a ton of fear. I was concerned about how things would work out. I hated the situation and the *reasons* for the situation. I hate that Craig and so many others hurt. I hate that Eric was in so much pain. But I mostly didn't think he'd kill me. Or at least I didn't think he wanted to kill me. What he might have done in an unstable moment is anyone's guess." Liam shifted on his sore ankle. "But I think I'd like to get whatever medical attention you think I need and then go home."

Drake pulled back and lifted Liam's chin. "Home?"

Liam smiled sleepily, the day clearly catching up with him. "Home. Wherever you are. That's my home. Always."

Drake returned the smile and kissed him softly. "And my home is forever with you."

EPILOGUE

Liam

A KNOCK SOUNDED at Liam's door. After peeking through the window, Liam opened the door with a huge smile on his face. "What are you doing here?" He threw himself into Drake's arms. "I thought we were meeting at your place after you got finished up at the office?"

Drake hugged him tight.

At the door, in plain sight, where anyone could see.

Oh, how things had changed.

"Well, I realized on my way home that I never once came to the door to pick you up for any of our dates and I wanted to change that before you don't have a door for me to come to." Drake nuzzled Liam's neck.

"Oh my God, you've turned into the biggest romantic sap," Liam teased. The day's job had been Liam packing up the remaining items he wanted to have with him at

Drake's place—his new *home*—until the movers could pack up the leftover big pieces that hadn't already been donated. Liam kissed Drake. "But I love it."

"And I love you." Drake returned the kiss. "You ready for our date?"

"I am. And I'm even more ready for our *two whole weeks* at the lake house." Liam checked his watch. "But we weren't scheduled to leave for dinner for two more hours."

Drake waggled his brow. "Pretty sure we can think of ways to fill the time." Then he scowled. "As long as your head is okay?"

Three days after the incident with Eric and getting a very small three stitches in his head to close up a tiny wound, Liam's head was no longer painful—although his heart still hurt for all that Eric had gone through that led him to do what he'd done.

"I'm good. Doctor said no restrictions unless my head was painful and it's not." Liam backed up and pulled Drake into the apartment. "One last time here for old time's sake?" He bit his lip and smiled.

Drake growled and kissed Liam hard.

When they broke apart, both breathless, Drake ran a thumb softly over Liam's lip. "So much as changed since way back then. And I'm so glad," he whispered.

"Show me how glad you are," Liam challenged as he stepped away and stripped his shirt over his head. "One last time here, on my couch. One more time at your place —*our* place—to welcome our new normal and celebrate our future." Liam popped the button on his jeans and pushed the material—underwear too—over his hips and stepped out of them. With a hand stroking his quickly lengthening cock, Liam licked his bottom lip. "You're over-dressed. Catch up, detective."

Drake ripped his clothes off and dropped to his knees. He gripped Liam's hips and opened his mouth to engulf Liam's already leaking dick.

Liam reached for Drake's head to steady himself. Fisting his hand in Drake's hair, Liam thrust his hips forward, reveling in the way Drake took his cock deep to the back of his throat.

When Drake fondled Liam's balls and teased his taint, Liam pulled back. "Don't want to come yet. Want you in me," he demanded as he walked to the couch and bent over the arm.

Drake knelt behind him, gripping Liam's ass cheeks and exposing his hole to Drake's probing, teasing tongue.

"Fuuuck," Liam cursed. "Feels so damn good." They'd had sex more than once since their unorthodox reunion on Cooper's land, but it had been gentle and loving and reassuring. Almost as if Drake was trying to make restitution for his behavior. But this was hot, dirty, and hopefully, rough sex that would have Liam's knees giving out and stars dancing in his head. "Fuck me," Liam begged.

Drake wasted no time soaking Liam's ass with spit, standing, slicking his dick, and slowly pressing the fat head of his cock into Liam's tight hole.

Liam whimpered with each burning, stretching inch and moaned when Drake's cock was fully inside. Liam's body rejoiced in the invasion and begged for release. "Move, please."

Drake gripped Liam's hips hard enough to leave marks and began to thrust hard and fast. "Get on your knees and push your ass back to me," Drake commanded.

Liam shifted so that he was knelt on his knees, perched on the side of the couch arm, his ass hanging off and ready for Drake to fill him again. He didn't have to wait long.

Drake pushed back in, wrapped one arm around Liam's waist and a fist around Liam's dick. "You wanna come?" Drake whispered as he nibbled and kissed along Liam's back.

"Fuck, yes," Liam hissed.

"Gonna come deep in your ass, so deep you'll feel it dripping even tonight on our date." Drake bit a sensitive spot on the side of Liam's torso. "All night, I'll think about my cum being deep in your ass. Then when we get home, I'll push my cock back inside you and you'll still be slick with it."

Liam groaned as Drake held him tight, fucking him hard, and stroking his cock. "Gonna come," Liam warned.

"Do it, come for me," Drake commanded.

Liam lost any control he pretended to have and shot his load in Drake's waiting fist.

Drake thrust once more, hard and fast, deep in Liam's ass as he roared his release.

Liam whimpered, his ass clenching around Drake's pulsing cock as warmth filled his body. "Fuck, so good," Liam whispered.

With a final kiss to Liam's back, Drake pulled out. "We should clean up just enough to get home, do *that* again, then shower and get ready for our date."

Liam agreed and moved from his spot on the couch. "I think I could get used to you coming to my door if it always leads to *that*. Too bad we'll be living together and have no need for you to pick me up."

Drake pulled Liam into his arms and kissed him deeply. "If you want to be picked up for every single date, I will leave and come to the door—hell, I'll bring flowers if you want them—as long as you'll have me."

"No one's ever brought me flowers," Liam mused against Drake's lips.

"Well then, flowers and coming to the door for dates it is. Get ready to be romanced."

"Yeah? You a romance expert now?" Liam teased even as his heart filled with love for the man he couldn't imagine living without.

"For you, I'll learn to be," Drake answered and kissed Liam again. "I love you more than life itself and I want to spend the rest of our lives proving my love to you."

"Only if I get to do the same." Liam cuddled into Drake's arms. "I think there are some paper towels for clean-up. We may be a little sticky on the drive home."

"Eh, it's okay. We'll just get messier before we jump into the shower." Drake smacked Liam's ass before they broke apart, cleaned up, and pulled on their clothes.

Drake picked up the final duffle bag Liam had packed and walked toward the door. Drake opened the door for Liam. "You ready?"

Liam took a quick glance around his apartment one last time. He looked forward to a simple date that evening, a two-week vacation at the lake house with Drake, and a future with the man he loved. Was he ready? Hell, yes. He was more than ready. "As long as you're by my side, loving me, I'm always ready."

Drake kissed him. "Then let's go."

Liam walked away from his past with a smile on his face and Drake holding his hand as they headed toward a happy, loving future.

THE END

PLEASE leave a review. Star ratings are GREAT! But a short little review (just a few words about what you liked/didn't like, how you felt, etc.) is soooo very helpful! You can review all of the titles you've read from me at author.to/ADEllisAmazon
Thank you!

Read on for more books from A.D. Ellis.

ALSO BY A.D. ELLIS

Silver in the City (3 books- meet the Silver crew you read about in Forged in the City) Available on AUDIO!

Forged in the City (3 books- a spin-off series from Silver in the City) Available on AUDIO

The BJ Boys Series (3 books, small town, big love) Available on AUDIO

Forever Better Together (friends to lovers) Coming soon to AUDIO!

His Reluctant Cowboy (age gap, opposites attract, cowboy romance) Available on AUDIO!

What Blooms Beneath (LGBT Fantasy romance) Available on AUDIO!

Sawyer

(this was the first M/M I wrote and you may remember Sawyer and Luke being mentioned in Barrett & Ivan as well as in Ryker & Gavin)

Start Something About Him with a **FREE** short story:

(The Beginning https://instafreebie.com/free/84Cxr)

Then continue with the other stand-alone titles in the series (available to read FREE for Kindle Unlimited subscribers):

Bryan & Jase

Brody & Nick

Barrett & Ivan

Braeton & Drew

Ryker & Gavin

Kade & Cameron

Or grab the boxset HERE.

———

Plus several other titles:

Devoted (a Something About Him novella)

Saving Us

Stranded Hearts (a short story)

Eli & Gage (a Something About Him short story)

———

A.D.'s first stories (all male/female except <u>Sawyer</u> which is male/male) are in the Torey Hope and Torey Hope: The Later Years series. Find the 8 book box set HERE or you can find each individual title on Amazon.

For Nicky

Because of Beckett

Christmas in Torey Hope

Loving Josie

Decker

Sawyer

Zach

Kendrick

ACKNOWLEDGMENTS

It's always so hard to write this part because I'm worried I'll forget someone without meaning to.

Readers- you are the reason I write. As long as you continue reading my stories, I'll continue writing them. Thank you for your support.

Bloggers- your support, reviews, and promotion are very much appreciated. Thank you!

My author buddies- I don't know that I could keep doing this without our brainstorm sessions, laughter, road trips, meals, wine, and friendship as my support.

Thank you to my betas, editors, proofreaders, and ARC readers! Your eyes and input are beyond important to me.

Brett and Gage- as usual, I doubt you even grasp how much your support, input, and friendship mean to me. This author journey has brought many wonderful things into my life, and you both are two of the BEST! I'm blessed to call you friends.

My family and friends- thank you for your love and support, always.

ABOUT THE AUTHOR

A.D. Ellis is an Indiana girl, born and raised. She spends much of her time in central Indiana as an instructional coach/teacher in the inner city of Indianapolis, being a mom to two amazing school-aged children, and wondering how she and her husband of almost two decades have managed to not drive each other insane. A lot of her time is also devoted to phone call avoidance and her hatred of cooking.

She loves chocolate, wine, pizza, and naps along with reading and writing romance. These loves don't leave much time for housework, much to the chagrin of her husband. Who would pick cleaning the house over a nap or a good book? She uses any extra time to increase her fluency in sarcasm.

Find all of Ellis' contemporary romance and male/male romance at www.adellisauthor.com

FREE books-- sign up at bit.ly/ADEllisNews for a FREE male/female romance.

Sign up at http://www.subscribepage.com/ADEllisNewsMMRomance for a FREE male/male romance book.